D1525814

THE LESS THAN SPECTACULAR TIMES OF HENRY MILCH

A Wyandot County Mystery

MARSHALL THORNTON

ENJOY!

Published by Kenmore Books

Edited by Joan Martinelli

Cover design by Marshall Thornton

Images by 123rf stock

ISBN: 979-8-63056-916-5

First Edition

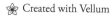 Created with Vellum

Acknowledgments

With great affection I'd like to thank Ben Starkey, Amy Barrett, Jeanie Williams, Tina Greene-Bevington, Robin Sinclair, Randy and Valerie Trumbull, and, of course, my editor Joan Martinelli.

Chapter 1

HOW I CAME to find a dead body on that crisp April morning is something of a puzzle. Truth be told, how I came to be in Northern Lower Michigan at all remains hard for me to grasp. Yes, yes, yes, I remember the facts of how it all happened. I was there after all. It's the *why* that's slippery. Chance and luck, mistakes and poorly thought-out decisions combined to lead me to that life-changing day, a day I still can't quite connect with.

The life I'd understood, the things I'd hoped for, planned for, worked for: college admission (UCLA), graduation (B.A., Communications), first job (barista), first apartment (East Hollywood with my best friend, Vinnie); that all felt like me. Like everyone else, I was climbing life's ladder. Things felt solid and real. It was all going as planned.

But then the other part, the part where swallowing an extra pill or two dropped me straight through a trap door with nowhere to land except a place I barely knew, far, far from anything that felt remotely like home. That's the slippery part. The part I have trouble with.

Anyway.

The assignment I'd been given that day was simple enough. In fact, the whole job was numbingly easy. I'd been sent to live with my Nana Cole—banished might be a better word—and it took three whole days before she tired of my moping and got me a part-time job with the Wyandot County Land Conservancy.

She volunteered for them one or two days a month, which I think was just an excuse to tease her close friend, Executive Director Bev Jenkins, with the possibility of including an easement on the family's thirty-five acre farm in her will. That interest in the eventual, and possibly imaginary, behest resulted in my working one or two days a week checking existing easements for compliance.

For weeks, I'd been stomping around snow-covered acreage, iPod blaring in my ears—Britney, Madonna, and, yes, I'll admit it *Mandy Moore*—taking photos of things I only kind of, barely understood. Bev seemed pleased though and only had to send me back to the same parcel once for a redo. I was, apparently, a big improvement over the honor student who'd been doing it right up until she got early acceptance at U of M in January.

Anyway, that particular day—April Fools' no less—The Conservancy received an anonymous note tacked to the door saying there were a couple of rusted-out, abandoned vehicles on the Sheck property out on Route 669, also called Old Farm to Market Road, which sliced Wyandot County in half like a craggy surgical scar. Abandoned vehicles were not only a violation of the easement but also of the law since the Sheck property was just inside Masons Bay Township. The Village of Masons Bay was different from the Township, something that was still baffling me after six weeks. A village was inside a township inside a county. It was geography demonstrated by Russian nesting dolls.

I drove out on Old Farm to Market Road listening to Britney's "Oops, I Did It Again" on my iPod. It was like my personal anthem and I occasionally—well, often, had it on repeat. My mood was good since I was pretty sure I'd be getting the Shecks into double trouble. The idea of someone else being on the hot seat pleased me more than it should have.

Maybe that makes me a terrible person, I don't know. Sometimes I'm not so sure I know what a terrible person is. I mean, there are so many terrible people pretending to be good that it's hard to be sure. Seriously, life should come with a manual. A really thick one.

And—I got lost. I usually did. Nana Cole let me drive her old truck: a red 1985 Ford F-150, which was a super simple vehicle with none of the bells and whistles cars and trucks come with today in 2003. It had a gas station map of the state in the glove compartment and I had to take it out to get to wherever I was supposed to go. Not surprisingly, I'd driven right past the Sheck place. Very few of the roads in Wyandot County were big enough to make the state map after all.

The county is on the west side of the state and shaped like a crumbling piece of pie between Leelanau and Benzie counties. When you live in Michigan, one of the things you pick up is that people like to hold up a hand and use it as a map. Detroit is underneath the thumb, Bay City is in the nook between the thumb and the index finger, Mackinaw is on the tip of the middle finger, and Northport is at the tippy top of the pinkie. If you want to tell someone where Wyandot County is, it's the wart at the bottom of the pinkie.

By the way, the residents of Wyandot County pronounce it *wine-dot*, which is probably not even remotely correct. The story I read about the county, which I found on Yahoo!, was that Wyandot was at one time another name for the Huron Nation. They were located in Eastern Michigan, down into Ohio and up into Canada. In the 1840s, the Wyandot people were relocated to Kansas. Famously, chief Big Turtle wrote letters back to midwestern journals saying the Wyandot were much better off in Kansas. Seriously? Was anyone *ever* better off in Kansas?

In the 1850s when the county was formed by William Bellflower, Charles Mason and Alexander Beckett, they named it Wyandot County in order to mock the remaining Native Americans, not-so-subtly suggesting they too would be happier in Kansas. It didn't exactly work, and there are now three different tribes running seven different casinos in Northern Lower Michigan—all happily, and legally, picking the pockets of the so-called founders' descendants.

After making a U-turn and heading back a quarter of a mile,

I pulled off onto the shoulder. The Sheck house fronted on Apple Lane over on the far side of the property. Per the parcel map I'd been given, there was a kind of gully or ditch on the Old Farm to Market Road side with a stream running through it. That's where the note said the cars would be found.

The sky was gray and heavy, reminding me of a water balloon hanging over my head ready to pop. Old Farm to Market Road was dusty with the sand snowplows had thrown onto it all winter. Patches of dingy snow showed up here and there like crusty white scabs. This was not the pretty, bright spring they showed in toilet paper commercials. Mostly, it was dirty, damp and dead-looking, making the idea of spring seem nearly impossible.

I switched the iPod over to classic Madonna but then got all tangled up in the earbuds while I was trying to use a small brass compass and the parcel map to find this gully née ditch. Oh, how the mighty had fallen. I used to spend my time deciding between Rage or Revolver and begging DJs to play more Kylie. Now, I looked for ditches.

Shaking those thoughts off, I pondered a stand of trees thick with dead underbrush: pines, birches, poplars. I stared at the compass trying to remember exactly how it worked. I was guessing the stream was to my right, which was south or maybe east. I saw what might be a path and decided the best thing to do was follow that.

Folding up the parcel map, and cramming it and the compass into my pocket with my iPod, I set off into the woods looking for the gully/ditch. Along the muddy path were a lot of snags—a word that was new to me, meaning dead trees still standing—creepy if you thought about it too long. I tried not to.

There were also a lot of dead trees rotting on the moist ground. I don't think you called those snags. They were simply dead trees rotting on the ground.

I hadn't gone far before I began wondering how someone would get a couple of old cars out there. There were a lot of trees in the way—dead and otherwise. Not to mention, if the cars were still running well enough to drive them into the woods, why abandon them?

Up this way, there were often old abandoned cars out in people's yards. Usually they appeared to arrive at their final destination in an organic way. Like you could imagine a farmer saying, 'Just park the Impala behind the barn, we'll get around to fixing her later.' And then later never comes, the Impala sinks into the ground, now windowless, grass growing through rusted floorboards, and presto chango they've got a junkyard out back.

But none of that fit with a couple of cars ending up in the Sheck's gully/ditch and I was beginning to think I was being punked, like in that new Ashton Kutcher show Vinnie told me about. One of the many shows I was missing out on since Nana Cole stubbornly refused to get cable.

I was lucky. The path did lead to the gully/ditch, but I didn't see any rusty old cars. I did see a lot of brown water. The snowmelt had filled up the stream that wound through it in the summer. Now it was gone, and in its place a shallow, narrow, murky pond. So, maybe it wasn't a gully or a ditch. At least not anymore.

Was this part of the Sheck place wetlands? It was definitely wet enough. And that might be why they'd been put under easement. Wetlands were important environmentally, don't ask me why exactly but I'd picked up that much at The Conservancy. To me, they looked like they'd be a hassle to develop anyway. You'd have to fill them up with dirt and the water would still have to go somewhere. And if you didn't put down enough dirt, then everyone's cellar would fill up in the spring just like the gully/ditch and that couldn't be good.

And all that water would probably make a mess of any sewer system. No, to me it seemed a lot easier to build on higher, dryer ground. Or better yet, move to the city.

I tromped around in the muck for a bit, still no cars. Then I took my flip phone out of my cheap blue puffer coat and called Bev.

"Is this an April fool's joke?" I asked when she picked up. "I'm not seeing any old cars out here."

"Well, it's not a joke. At least not one I'm playing."

"What did the note say again?"

"Hold on." She set the phone down and I waited a bit for her to come back. The birds were out, making noise. Nana Cole knew them by sound. If she were with me she'd be saying, 'That's a cardinal. That's a chick-a-dee.' I had no idea which was which. I just thought they were all viciously loud.

Bev came back to the phone. "Your grandmother called. She wants you to pick up a loaf of bread and maybe some muffins at Beanie's Bakery on your way home."

"Okay," I said. I could have asked why she just didn't call me herself, but that would have been pointless, I knew. Nana Cole couldn't get used to the idea that my mother had found us a family cell phone plan that didn't charge per minute. She just couldn't get used to the idea that a thirty-second phone call here and there wouldn't land you in bankruptcy court.

Not to mention, it was my mom's dime not hers, so she shouldn't even care. But none of that mattered; she was just too terrified to call me on the cell.

"All right. The note just says, 'There are a couple of old cars on the southeast corner of the Sheck place by the stream.'"

"It's a lot more than a stream right now."

"You think this is someone's idea of a joke?" she asked.

"It's not very funny."

"Did you walk the whole stream?"

"I'm about half way down. I think." Was I? I wasn't exactly a pro at reading maps.

"Walk the rest just to be sure."

"Okay," I said, without mentioning I thought it was a waste of time. I flipped the phone shut and slipped it into my pocket.

I stood there a moment, thinking I might just turn around. I wasn't going to find any cars and Bev would never know, right? I decided to split the difference. I'd go another hundred feet or so and call it a day. The ground was covered in soggy, squishy, mucky leaves that had dropped the fall before. While I was being vaguely disgusted, I managed to scare a rabbit and it bounced off deeper into the trees. The undergrowth looked dead but was, apparently, ready to spring back to life. Walking along the gurgling stream/pond, I noticed there was more snow this far in. Big, icy mounds on both sides of the water.

It was noticeably colder, too, and darker. From the map, it seemed like I was almost to the end of the stream as it meandered off onto the neighbor's property. Maybe—or was I reading it wrong?

That's when I noticed a reddish-brown loafer on the ground. Penny loafer. At first, it looked like someone had thrown it away. But why would someone throw away a single shoe out here? And a new shoe at that. Then I saw the other one, partially buried in the snow. I stepped closer. There was an ankle coming out of the first shoe, an ankle that had been gnawed down to the bone. Disgusting. Above the wound, was a glimpse of a shredded argyle sock, the hem of a pair of jeans. Then the body disappeared under the snow. The mound of crunchy, dingy snow laying in front of me took on a whole new meaning.

Backing up, I realized I hadn't taken a breath in a long time. I started back out to Route 669 walking at first and then running. Running didn't help with my non-breathing, especially through the muddy, mucky… I had to bend over and catch my breath when I got to the road. A minute or so later, when I was breathing more like a human being, I took out my phone and dialed 911.

It rang. And rang. And rang.

Vaguely, I remembered there were sometimes problems with cell phones and 911, especially this far out. The calls didn't always go through. I hung up and called Bev again.

"Um."

"Henry?" Bev said. "That you?"

"Um, yeah."

"Did you find those cars?"

"No. I found a body."

"A what?"

"A man's body. Could you call 911? I tried but it didn't work."

"Are you okay?"

7

"I don't know. I guess."

"You're still at the Sheck place?"

"Uh-huh. On Old Farm to Market Road *behind* the Sheck place."

"Okay. Stay there."

The road was quiet. I didn't think anyone had driven by while I was out in the muck. It was cold with a bit of wind. I decided I'd be happier waiting inside the F-150. When I got in, I turned on the engine so I could warm-up. Then I pulled out my wallet. Inside was a folded-up piece of paper, which I took out and opened up. Inside were three round, blue pills: Diazepam. AKA Valium, 10 mg. I broke one in half and swallowed it. I'd found the pills in Bev's purse the day I got the job. I'd been saving them for a special occasion. Stumbling upon a dead body seemed kind of special.

A couple of cars went by while I waited. They weren't the cops. Then, in the distance, I saw flashing lights. That seemed kind of pointless. Clearly, the crime had already been committed—probably quite some time ago given the thick blanket of snow. CPR wasn't going to do this guy a bit of good. Whoever this cop was, they were just showing off.

They pulled up. Ford Explorer. White with SHERIFF written on the side in a grassy green. There was a big black rack thing attached to the front grill. I had no idea what that was for, except maybe bashing down barn doors? I got out of the truck before the sheriff did. When he did, he left the lights flashing.

He was probably in his late fifties. Tall. Black uniform, tight in the middle. His green parka open. He wore a flat-brimmed hat, which left his ears open to the cold wind. A hat that didn't have any real purpose I could see.

When he got close he said, "Sheriff Dill Crocker." He didn't hold out his hand or anything. It sounded like an accusation. "You Henry?"

I flinched, since I hated the name, and said, "Yeah. People call me Mooch."

"Do they?" he said in a way that told me he'd never call me

that. Which seemed ridiculous since his name was Dill. "You Emily Cole's kid?"

"Fetterman. She's Emily Fetterman now."

"And Emma Cole is your grandmother?"

"Yeah, she is."

People up there like to establish your family tree before they begin a conversation. If you were related to one of the old families, like the Masons or the Shecks or the Becketts, you were afforded respect. If you were new to the area—and that meant anything less than a hundred years—you got less respect. And if you were a fudgie—the name given to the tourists and snowbirds who supported the fudge shops that were in every single itty-bitty town like Masons Bay—well, you didn't get any respect at all.

"We've had four prank calls this morning," Sheriff Crocker said.

"It's not a prank."

"You seem awfully calm for someone who's just seen a dead body."

"Um, I kind of only saw his shoes." The Valium had kicked in and I wasn't shaking anymore, but I could hardly tell him that.

"Shoes? Am I going to walk out there and find a pair of shoes?"

"Ankles. I saw his ankles too. He's under some snow."

An old blue Subaru wagon pulled to a stop behind Nana's truck. It had a little rust on the back fender and one of those small American flags that clipped onto the passenger door. The kind everyone in L.A. flew on their cars right after 9/11.

A man in his early forties wearing a pair of jeans, a dingy white thermal T-shirt, and jean jacket got out of the Subaru. He marched over and asked Sheriff Crocker, "This ain't a joke, is it?"

"He says not."

"Who is he?"

"Henry Fetterman. Emma Cole's grandson."

"Milch," I said to the sheriff. "Henry Milch. My mother has

a different name." She'd had many names, but that's another story.

The other man looked me up and down like he was trying to identify roadkill. "What's he doing out here?"

"You work for Bev, right?"

"At The Wyandot Land Conservancy, yes."

"Bev's good people," the sheriff said. "This is our detective, Rudy Lehmann. Used to work down in Grand Rapids."

"All right, Henry," Detective Lehmann said. "Show us where this body is."

I led them off the road and onto the Sheck property. None of us said anything as we walked along the path. When we got to the overflowing stream, I said, "It's down near the far end of the stream."

Not that there really was an end to the stream, it was just the end of the stream on the Sheck's property. I almost said that but was afraid I'd sound like I was babbling. Neither of them cared where the stream ended. For that matter, neither did I.

Moments later we were standing next to the corpse. Detective Lehmann bent over the mound of snow and carefully brushed it away from what should be the man's face. When he got enough of it brushed away he said, "Yup. Sammy Hart." Apparently, critters had not gotten to Sammy's face.

The sheriff nodded.

"Who is that?" I asked.

"Disappeared in February," Detective Lehmann said.

"Suicide?" the sheriff asked.

"Maybe."

"No," I said, before I could stop myself. Actually, before I even thought about it.

The sheriff stared at me. "What do you mean, no?"

"Um," I said, rather inarticulately.

"He has no idea," Lehmann said.

"We got a note," I blurted. "An anonymous note that said there were some old cars out here along the stream. That's what I was doing out here."

"Yeah, so what?" The detective was not impressed.

In fact, it was obvious I was annoying him. I should have shut my mouth. I didn't.

"There are no cars. So why did someone leave that note?"

"April fools."

"Or they wanted someone to find this guy. Don't you think?"

Chapter 2

WHEN I FIRST crash-landed in Michigan, I took a long look around my nana's farm. It had been more than a decade since I'd been there and, well, I didn't have anything else to do. So, I looked around. A lot.

In the front, along West Shore Road, on the west side of our driveway, there were around five acres of neatly arranged, recently planted cherry trees. In February, they were craggy stick figures popping out of the snow. The bottom part of the trunk had been painted white up to about three feet. That must have improved health or production or flavor. I've never asked which or even what that white stuff is. In fact, the orchard was never much of a concern to me.

Along the other side of our driveway was another orchard, this one mature, taking up about ten or twelve acres. My grandmother leased both out to her neighbor to the east, Jasper Kaine. He had his own twenty acres of cherry trees, so it wasn't much bother to take care of Nana Cole's and he paid her half his profit on the acreage. It was a good deal for both of them.

Her house—clapboard, two-stories with a big old stone porch—sat behind the orchard. There were a couple of outbuildings; one a workshop and the other a red pole barn for the cars and farm equipment—most of which she didn't use anymore.

Then there were a couple of acres down a sloping hill where Nana planted vegetables every year: cabbage for slaw, squash, lots of squash, carrots, garlic and some onions. I knew all this because much of what she fed me came with comments about last summer's crop: carrots were good, acorn squash dry and stringy.

Beyond the vegetable garden were four rows of raspberry bushes she'd strung up years ago—these I remembered from childhood visits. They just needed to be picked in late July. There was an overgrown chicken coup; she'd kept chickens for a decade or so but found them to be annoying, nasty animals who were much more appealing wrapped in Styrofoam and plastic.

At the very back of the property, down a rolling hill where she'd once grown rows and rows of corn, were ten or fifteen acres of trees and a small, kidney-shaped pond. She was good with a rifle and, in season, would go out into those woods to shoot a deer or a wild turkey. She'd dress the deer out there in the woods since she couldn't carry it. When she'd finished, she'd pile the meat into a child's wagon and pull it back to the house.

That was the part of the property that scared me most when I arrived. The woods. I can't tell you how many movies I've seen that start out with a city person visiting the country and ending up with that same guileless city person chopped to bits in some hillbilly's prize-winning chili. Those movies made a big impression on me, and were responsible for a number of frights in those first few weeks.

I'd lived in Los Angeles my whole life, so I kept locking doors. Nana Cole had a fit until she broke me of the habit. "You're safe. Nothing happens out here," she'd tell me. Truth be told, even though I'd spent my life locking doors I don't think anyone had ever actually come by and checked to see if I had. *And*, I knew perfectly well that any seasoned thief could get past a locked door in a flash. Still, the day I found the dead body, I was tempted to start locking doors again no matter what Nana Cole said.

Getting out of the truck, I walked around back to the kitchen door, but before I went in I whistled for Reilly. He was

Nana's six-year-old yellow Lab-mix and the one battle with her I'd won definitively. When I arrived, when it was frigidly cold—well, *more* frigidly cold than it was in April—Reilly was living in a grimy doghouse out by the vegetable garden. I brought him inside as soon as I saw it—actually, I brought him to a groomer near the mall in Bellflower and got him a bath and nail grind—and from then on he slept inside with me.

"People have stopped having children and now they treat animals like their own kids. It's not right. It's not how things were. A dog is a dog not a child." Those are the *CliffsNotes*. I probably listened to a couple hours of commentary about how dogs were treated when she was young—the right way—and how they were treated now—the wrong way.

She still put him out when I wasn't there, but when I came back he'd come when I called—as he did that day—and jump on me a couple times even though I told him no. I wasn't what anyone would call a dog person so discipline was little more than a concept, but he was a good dog, well-behaved. Most of the time.

When we walked into the kitchen, Nana Cole was sitting there with her friend, my boss, Bev. My nana was somewhere near seventy—one side or the other, I didn't know which—white-haired, rheumy-eyed, with skin as wrinkled as a used sheet of wax paper. Bev was younger, though by how much I couldn't tell. She had steely hair and a nose like a knife. I got out Reilly's bowl and filled it with water.

"D'you go to the bakery?" Nana Cole asked.

"I forgot."

"You forgot?"

"Dead bodies will do that to you." Though, it was probably the half a Valium I took. Or the whole one I took on the way home. "I'll go later."

"I wanted the bread for lunch."

I put the water down and let Reilly splash it around in what passed for taking a drink. Hopefully, some of it got in his mouth.

"Too bad there's nothing in the pantry," I said.

The pantry was the size of a bedroom in L.A. (or a whole New York City apartment from I hear) and was full of dry goods and canned vegetables from last year's garden. Not to mention, there were at least two loaves of bread that I was personally aware of in the freezer in the basement. Nana Cole was just partial to the sourdough at Beanie's Bakery.

"He was such a sweet child," she said to Bev. "I don't know what happened."

She passed that off as a joke, but I had the feeling she half meant it. Well, more than half.

I sat down and asked, "Who's Sammy Hart?"

"That who you found?" Bev asked.

I nodded.

Nana Cole said, "The Harts go back a ways, they owned an Italian restaurant in the village for a long while."

"Who'd they sell that to?" Bev wondered.

"Couple out of Chicago." Nana Cole shook her head as though no one in Chicago could run a business. "Only lasted a year or two. None of the locals would go there."

"Sammy's mother was a Beckett, wasn't she?" Bev asked.

Nana Cole nodded.

Even I knew who the Becketts were. They still had their name on a lot of things around Masons Bay: a farm, a construction company, a funeral parlor. I imagined Sammy would be getting a family and friends discount on his final purchase.

"That's right," Nana Cole said. "He was Colleen's boy. Odd, never married."

"Yup, that's the one."

There was an uncomfortable silence—or at least it was uncomfortable for me. We listened to the kitchen clock tick. Something wasn't being said, something obvious. These were code words. Never married. Odd. Sammy Hart was gay. *Well that figures,* I thought, *the first gay person I meet in Michigan is a corpse.*

Reilly was done lapping up water and hovered around my knees. I told him to lie down and he went and lay in the big squishy bed I'd gotten him. I don't think he was minding me, though, I think we just happened to agree that he should lie down.

"They want me to come in tomorrow and make a statement," I said. "And I'm supposed to bring the note with me."

"What note?" Nana Cole asked.

"That's why I was at the Sheck's. There was a note."

Bev continued for me, "Someone tacked it to the door, oh, last night or this morning. Said there were some old cars out at the Sheck's didn't belong."

"There weren't though," I pointed out.

"So, it *was* a prank."

"Well, no, I don't think so," I said. "I think maybe someone wanted us to find the body."

"Oh you watch too much TV," Nana said.

"I would if you'd get cable."

"Then you'd do nothing but sit around like a couch potato."

Which wasn't far from what I'd been doing on my days off even without movie channels and MTV. And *The Real World.*, God I missed *The Real World*. Without cable, I did have a DVD player on my iBook and there was a Hometown Video on the way to Bellflower. I'd already become very familiar with their stock. Very, very middle-of-the-road, FYI.

"It doesn't make sense that someone would kill Sammy Hart, go to the trouble of hiding him at the Sheck's, and then tell us where he was," Bev said, then sipped her coffee.

"They might have killed him there," I said.

Had they? I wondered. *Was there a way to figure it out?*

"Why kill him out there, though?" Bev asked.

I shrugged. "So you wouldn't have to carry him? It did seem like a long way to carry someone."

"It's got to be a coincidence. Someone actually thought there were cars out there," Bev said. "I mean, why not send the note to the police? Why get us involved?"

I shrugged again. "I don't know. But I bet there's a reason."

Nana Cole stood up. "Well, I'd better find something for lunch. You staying, Bev?"

"No, I should go out and talk to the Shecks. If I know Lou

Sheck, he's going to try and find a way to blame this on The Conservancy."

She stood up to leave.

"I've got some bagels," Nana Cole said. "I can make you a sandwich on a bagel. You sure you don't want one to go?"

"No thanks." She gave my grandmother a little hug and was out the door. Nana Cole started unloading sandwich fixings from the refrigerator.

"I know you won't go to church with me, but there's a pancake supper tomorrow. I want you to go. My friends don't believe you exist."

"Your friends know I exist." I'd met enough of them just going into Masons Bay with her.

"Well, you like pancakes, don't you?"

"Are you trying to turn pancakes into a gateway drug to Jesus?"

"That's not funny."

"It wasn't a joke."

She stopped what she was doing. For a moment, she was quiet enough that I knew I'd stepped in it. Again. I stepped in it a lot.

"The dinner's at seven. Make sure you're ready by six-thirty. And you can make your own damn sandwich."

With that she left the kitchen.

————

I HAVE to get out of here, I thought for like the hundredth time that week. Masons Bay was not where I belonged. And, for about the hundredth time that week, I could not figure out a way to leave. Leaving required money and, tragically, I had very little of that.

The room I was staying in had been my mother's when she was growing up. Nana Cole hadn't changed it much. It still had the same lilac walls and a yellowing David Cassidy poster over her desk. The furniture was wooden but painted glossy white. I kind of remembered my mother telling a story about getting it all at an unfinished furniture store and painting it herself. It was about time to repaint it—it had chipped in places and was dirty in others—but there was no way I was doing that.

I lay on the bed with Reilly, feeding him part of my sandwich when I got bored with eating it. The bed was a twin, so there was barely enough room for both of us. I took out my flip phone, scrolled through my contacts and hit my former roommate's name, VINNIE.

"Moochie! How are you, baby?" he croaked when he picked up.

"Did I wake you up?" I'd forgotten to calculate the time difference. It was ten in the morning in L.A.

"Don't worry, it's okay. Come on, sweetie, tell me how you are? How are things in the land of fat white people?"

I cringed a little. Yes, I'd told him I was in the land of fat white people right after I'd gotten there—and it was kind of true. It just sounded so much meaner when someone else said it.

"I found a dead body."

He took that right in stride. "Forgive me if I don't act surprised. Was it a relative?"

"No. Just some guy."

"You didn't have anything to do with his ending up dead, did you?"

"Vinnie! Of course not. You've known me long enough to know which laws I'd break and which I wouldn't."

"That's true. I guess if you really needed someone dead you'd call me."

"Exactly," I said, though I knew perfectly well he wouldn't hurt a fly. Actually, he took particular relish in killing flies. But he wouldn't hurt a *human being*.

"Speaking of people you might kill," I said. "How's the roommate?"

"Still alive."

"You don't like him any better?"

"I like that he pays half the rent."

"I'm sorry," I couldn't help saying. "I know I messed up."

"You've apologized a dozen times. Only a few more times and you can stop."

I *had* really left him in the lurch. We were sharing a decrepit two-bedroom in the Hollywood flats with each of us paying six hundred a month. That—given our basically crappy jobs—his as waiter, mine as a barista—was a lot of money. My mother, well, her boyfriend, paid an extra month's rent when I was banished to Northern Lower Michigan and then, in the nick of time, Vinnie found his new roommate, Carlos. Carlos was the friend of a friend of a friend and the best he could do on short notice.

"If I win the lottery, I'll come home," I said.

"Did you buy a ticket?"

"No."

"Darling, you're not going to win then. Go to the 7-Eleven immediately. Wait do you even have 7-Elevens?"

"I think so." I wasn't sure. It had been a while since I'd seen one. "There might be one in Bellflower. Definitely over in Traverse City."

"It's not civilized unless there's one every few blocks. What about Starbucks?"

"I haven't seen one. I mean, there are coffee places just not Starbucks." I knew Masons Bay had a crazy rule against franchise places, maybe some of the other—

"What do people do?"

He meant what do people do without Starbucks, but I ignored that and said, "Tomorrow I have to go to a pancake supper at my grandmother's church."

"A dead body *and* a pancake supper in the same week? Do you need me to send you a care package?"

"No. Do *not* do that. My grandmother would open it."

"Get a P.O. Box."

"She knows everyone at the post office."

"Oh my, I wonder what that would be like." The post office in Hollywood always seemed to be filled with overworked unhappy people you never wanted to see again and generally never did. He continued, "I'm devastated that I can't do anything for you."

"It's okay." Anything Vinnie would send in a care package was likely to be a federal crime anyway.

"So have you met anyone? I mean, anyone living."

"I checked out the chat rooms. Everyone up here is either ugly, married or sixteen pretending to be twenty-one."

"Yuck."

"I know."

"What are you going to do?"

"I don't know. Seriously, I really don't know."

"Poor thing."

Chapter 3

LATE THE NEXT MORNING, I went to the Wyandot County Municipal Center where the sheriff's office was located to give my statement. First though, I stopped at The Conservancy office in Masons Bay—it was on Main Street in an old gray house that had been divided into office space—and picked up the letter from Bev. I'd brought an extra-large Ziploc bag from Nana Cole's kitchen and had Bev put it directly inside. We didn't want to get any more fingerprints on it than we needed to.

The Municipal Center was just outside of Masons Bay off Duck Pond Road. Three recently constructed, modern brick buildings circled a large parking lot—not unlike pioneer wagons protecting themselves from marauding Indians in a Hollywood western. From the signage, I learned that the Municipal Center housed several courts, the county clerk, the sheriff and the county commissioners. Basically, everything that had to do with running the county. Not that I knew much about running counties.

The sheriff's office was sparsely populated. I wasn't sure exactly how many people worked in the department, I supposed not many. And the officers they did have were probably out keeping an eye on the county, arresting speeders and other vaguely important things.

I was standing in a large room filled with a half-dozen

empty-looking desks. Around the edges of the room were several offices, also empty. I did hear a TV, though, and followed the sound until I discovered a conference room. Inside, Sheriff Crocker and Detective Lehmann were watching *9&10 Morning News*. It appeared to be from that same morning—I'd slept soundly through it—because Sheriff Crocker was being interviewed by a reporter about the deceased, formerly missing, Bellflower man. He was giving a terrible interview, using far too many words to say that Sammy Hart had been killed by a blow to the head around the time he disappeared in February. When the interview finished, Sheriff Crocker said, "Play it again."

I cleared my throat. *I* certainly didn't need a rerun.

"Oh, you're here. Good," Detective Lehmann said. He handed the remote to the sheriff and told me to follow him.

Back out in the big room, he walked me over to an empty desk. I held out the anonymous note in its Ziploc bag. He took it.

"Did you touch it?"

"No. I think Bev is the only one who touched it."

He nodded. He opened up one of the desk drawers and pulled out a sheet of paper. Handing it to me, he said, "Just write down what happened yesterday when you went out to the Sheck's. You can stop right before you called 911."

He walked away, and I looked down at the sheet. It might have been a special Microsoft Word template. It said, WITNESS STATEMENT toward the top of the page. To one side, it said WYANDOT COUNTY SHERIFF'S OFFICE and on the other was the address of the building we were in. Also, a whole bunch of phone numbers.

Then there were a lot of blanks for me to fill out. My name, address, phone, mobile phone, employer, their address and phone numbers, what I did for them and the number from my Driver's License. Underneath, they'd been kind enough to type in "I, the undersigned, make the following statement voluntarily, without threat, duress, or promise of reward:" The fact they'd gone ahead and typed that up for me made me feel a little like that in itself was duress. I mean, *I* felt pressured.

But I hadn't done anything wrong, so it shouldn't have bothered me. I shuffled in my seat, took a deep breath and started writing. I wrote everything down as simply as I could without embellishment of any kind.

I could hear the TV still playing in the conference room. The sheriff had stopped watching himself and now seemed to be watching *FOX News*. I could hear the report about the marines invading Baghdad. Apparently, it was going well. This was the shock and awe that we'd been promised, I mean they'd been promised, someone had been promised.

Nana Cole would be pleased. Even though I didn't think it was true, she'd gotten it in her head that Saddam Hussein was behind 9/11. So she found it incredibly satisfying to know he was about to be brought to justice.

I asked her to explain that theory to me once and she said a bunch of things that didn't really connect. I'd have worried she was suffering from dementia but, if she were, it was an epidemic. It seemed like half the world believed things that were actually wrong. I mean *obviously* wrong.

I'd tried explaining that Osama bin Laden and the hijackers were all Saudis, but that just got me, "Same hand, different finger." Which, honestly, was like saying America had to take responsibility for whatever England or France or even Russia did since we were all mostly white and Christian. Didn't make sense. Did it?

I tried to focus on my statement. It was very simple. We got a note. I went to check it out. I found a body. The hard part was trying to figure out if they wanted more than that. Should I describe where the body was? Should I talk about what he wearing? Well, what his feet were wearing since I didn't really see much else. The loafers were kind of nice. Nearly new, I think. Should I mention that?

As I was deliberating, three people came into the room: two old men and a girl around my age. The girl was chunky around the hips and had orange hair in a buzz cut. I wanted to roll my eyes. Jelly bean-colored hair was so 1980s. In some of my baby pictures my mother had streaks of pink in her hair. I mean, I guess some people still thought it was cool, or retro, but it was hardly original.

They were all dressed for the weather: sweaters and light raincoats. The two old guys were in their fifties with the fey, beaten look of longtime English teachers. One of them even carried a stack of papers and it looked like he might hand them out. Next week's assignment.

"Sheriff Crocker," the one with the assignments called out. They hadn't even reached the sheriff's office. A moment, later Sheriff Crocker stood in his doorway.

"You know, I don't have a lot of time to talk to you today."

"Really? Really? You've got plenty of time to talk to the press."

"And what you saw on TV is all I can tell you. We found Sammy Hart's body out on the Sheck property. He'd been hit on the head."

"When? When did it happen?"

"Roughly about the time he disappeared. He's been out there in the snow so it's a little hard to pinpoint exactly—"

"So he could have been alive while you were sitting on your hands doing nothing?" There was horror on the man's face, he seemed about a millisecond away from completely losing it.

"I don't think that's what happened," Detective Lehmann said, coming out of his office and speaking calmly. "There's no indication he was held for any length of time. His clothes weren't ripped or torn or even especially dirty. If he'd been held against his will for any length of time there would be wear on his clothing, don't you think?"

It made sense to me, but the looks on the trio's faces suggested they didn't want to believe it.

"We found him for you," the sheriff said. "You're going to have to be happy with that for the moment."

"You didn't find him. He fell into your lap."

Then the other guy spoke, "Richard, just stop. They're not going to admit they did anything wrong. They're not going to apologize. We should just say what we came to say and get out of here."

Richard, the one who'd been doing most of the talking, took a deep breath and said, "Look, we've raised fifteen thousand dollars. We're offering it as a reward for information leading to the capture of Sammy's killer."

"You should have talked to me—"

"We did talk to you. You weren't any help."

The other guy said, "We've brought some flyers for you. If you could give them out to people that would be great."

The sheriff frowned. It didn't seem likely he'd pass the flyers around.

The guy set the flyers down and turned to Richard, "Let's get out of here before this gets any uglier."

The three of them tromped out. I realized the girl hadn't said a word. I wondered who she was. Richard and the other guy were probably friends of Sammy's, they were around the same age. But who was she?

I tried to finish my statement, but my hand was shaking. Slowly, I was beginning to understand something. Fifteen thousand dollars could solve a lot of my problems. Not all of them— I hadn't even gotten the hospital bill from the two days I was locked in there—but it might solve enough of my problems that I could get back to L.A. It might get me home. I finished my statement and brought it over to Detective Lehmann's office.

"You done?" he asked when he saw me there.

I nodded, stepping into the office and handing him the statement.

"Thank you for coming in and doing this."

I felt like I should try to find out a little more before I left, so I asked, "Do you know whether Mr. Hart was killed where I found him?"

"I can't talk about the case."

Then I felt stupid. Not because he couldn't talk about the case. That was no surprise. I felt stupid because it was so obvious Sammy Hart wasn't killed out there. He was wearing loafers and they looked like they were in pretty good shape.

One of the first things Nana Cole did when I arrived in February was take me over to the Meijer in Traverse City and make me buy—in addition to a discounted, blue puffer jacket —a huge, chunky pair of rubberized winter boots. Otherwise my shoes would have been ruined in about five minutes. Sammy Hart would never have been walking around on the Sheck property in those loafers. And anyway, they didn't look ruined. If he *had* walked out there the heat from his feet would have melted the snow that got on his shoes and they'd have been ruined. Someone had to have carried him out there. And he was probably already dead.

"Can you tell me how big Sammy Hart was?" I asked.

"Why do you need to know that?"

"I don't—I mean, I'm just curious. I guess I can ask someone else."

"He was about six two and weighed a good two-twenty, two thirty."

"Thanks," I said and walked out. I could feel him watching me suspiciously as I left. On the way, I snagged one of the flyers about the reward. It was printed on a goldenrod-colored piece of copy paper. It had a black-and-white picture of Sammy Hart —well, black and goldenrod. He'd obviously been an attractive guy, at least at one point. In the picture, he was solid, distinguished, kind of like an old Leonardo DiCaprio. A very old Leonardo DiCaprio. In Hollywood, they'd have cast him as the CEO, the generous father, the kindly coach. Secondary roles, character parts.

Still, Sammy looked like he'd been a happy guy. At least until someone bonked him over the head. Under the picture, it just said he was everyone's friend and they'd raised fifteen thousand dollars to give to someone for information leading to the arrest of his killer. That was perfect. It wasn't like I'd have to actually catch the killer. All I'd have to do was find information that would lead to his arrest. That didn't sound dangerous. Or even that hard.

As I drove back to Nana Cole's, I listened to Pink get her party started on my iPod and tried to figure out if one person could carry a man the size of Sammy Hart. I suppose a fireman could. There was such a thing as a fireman's carry, right? How that worked I wasn't sure. And maybe you actually did have to be a fireman. Or at least pretty strong.

I was trying to figure out if the killer had had an accomplice. As nearly as I could tell there were two kinds of accomplices. Okay, there were probably more than two, but there were two that I was thinking of. There was the kind you called in advance and said, "Hey, I'm thinking of killing Sammy Hart wanna help?" And then there was the kind you called afterward and said, "Hey, I just killed Sammy Hart. Wanna help move the body?"

Like, if I knew why Sammy was killed then I could figure out what kind of accomplice the killer had. If it was a spontaneous crime of passion, then the killer probably used his phone-a-friend to get help. Vinnie was my phone-a-friend. I mean, we decided that once while watching *Who Wants to Be a Millionaire*. I think it applied to dead bodies too. Not that Vinnie would *plan* a murder with me. But he'd be much more forgiving if I killed someone in a moment of passion. None of this told me much, except that the killer had friends. Possibly better friends than I did.

When I pulled up behind the pole barn, Reilly came running. He jumped on me, covering me in mud. He'd been in the pond. Again. The ice was melting around the edges and he loved to drink from it, which generally necessitated standing in four inches of water. I pushed him off and said, "Come on, boy. Come on, Reilly."

It was just after noon; Nana Cole would be listening to Rush Limbaugh on the radio, so I decided to take Reilly for a good long walk. I usually did that at noon. Even in the snow. There were days when I'd take him out back toward the garden. I didn't need to tromp out very far before he was running circles around me. If the snow was deep and recent, I'd take Reilly up and down the driveway. It was a long driveway and Nana Cole always had it plowed. Out to the 22 and back usually took about as long as Limbaugh's show.

But now the snow was gone so we walked down by the gardens. The grass was pasted to the ground. A surprising amount of it was green from the year before. Apparently, it didn't have to die off completely to get through the winter. The day was warm—well, Michigan warm—up in the forties and the birds had come out. It was noisy.

Reilly bounced around, running ahead of me and then coming back. Turning every so often to keep an eye on me. Nana Cole said he had a lot of energy for a dog his age, but I think it was really that he'd been mostly ignored for a long time, so the least bit of attention got him jumping around.

I knew that Nana Cole liked Reilly, loved him even, it was just that she had a whole different idea about what dogs were for. She thought they were meant to be outside barking at anything that moved or going out into the woods and chasing down the things she shot. I thought he was there to be my friend.

Once I got down by the compost pile, I started thinking about the reward money again. I needed a car. I could buy one in Michigan and drive it back to California. Obviously, that would be a lot of the money. Maybe half the reward. I'd had car in California. Everyone had a car. Mine was a 1990 Honda CRX. But when I had my supposed overdose, my mother took it away, which was really unfair since she'd given it to me. Yes, her name was still on the title but that was just so the insurance was cheaper. The fact that she'd taken my car back, slapped a 5150 on me and then manipulated me into coming to live with my grandmother were just a few of the many, many reasons we weren't on speaking terms.

So, I would need to buy a good used car. One that would make it back to Los Angeles and then not give me much trouble for a couple of years. I also needed to catch up on my student loan, which was probably two thousand dollars behind. If I paid six or seven month's rent in advance, there would be just enough left for a really fun shopping trip or a stop in Las Vegas.

I wouldn't be paying a single dime for my trip to the hospital, but I hadn't wanted to go in the first place. And I certainly hadn't wanted to stay there against my will for three very expensive days. Once I was back in Los Angeles, I could either tell them to send the bill to my mother or explain that I was indigent and without insurance—the reward would be gone by then —so maybe they wouldn't even send me a bill. I mean, what would be the point, right?

All I needed to do was figure out who killed Sammy Hart. How hard could that be?

Chapter 4

MY NANA COLE'S other vehicle was a black '99 Cadillac Escalade. She'd gotten it right after my grandfather died in 2000. I was pretty sure she had no idea it was exactly the kind of car the Crips and the Bloods drove around South-Central L.A.—and I was nice enough not to tell her.

See, I could be nice when I wanted to be.

Anyway, the SUV rode like a bubble bath. Ironically, it had OnStar—which was wasted on Nana Cole, since she barely knew how to use so it. It would *not* have been wasted on me, since the operators helped you out whenever you got lost, even if that was a daily occurrence. I did point that out to her once, but, sadly, I remained relegated to the old F-150.

We were on our way to the pancake supper—I was working up the nerve to ask her to turn off the god-awful country station she listened to—when she said, "Your mother called this morning. She'd love to talk to you."

"Uh-huh," I said, very noncommittal since I knew it was not going to happen. Actually saying that would have caused a fight, so best not to say anything.

"You can't *not* talk to her forever."

"She's almost forty. I don't think she's got forever." Oops. That was hardly noncommittal.

"That's not funny."

"Yes, it is. You just don't have a sense of humor."

"I did before you came," she said under her breath.

That almost made me smile. The idea that I was capable of annoying her was something I enjoyed. She annoyed me, so I was more than happy to return the favor.

Of course, it was weird that my mother and grandmother were talking to each other at all. In my lifetime, they'd never gotten along. Or at least that's what I'd always thought. I mean, I slept in a room that was unchanged from the time my mother was seventeen. That suggested Nana Cole missed my mother. Or maybe she missed the teenaged version. Well, my fourteen-year-old mother say, or maybe even the fifteen-year-old version. Certainly, she couldn't miss the seventeen-year-old who ran off and married Pauly Milch.

The marriage didn't last long, but it did get my mother to California. Several years later she had a casual affair—she refused to call it a one-night-stand since it had taken up an entire weekend—and I came along. She was still using her first husband's name, so I ended up with that. Occasionally she would tell me the name was more valuable than Pauly Milch's genetic material. Though, I could never see why. I would have been happy as Henry Cole. Or Henry whomever.

Anyway, somewhere along the line between the many marriages, frequent career changes and one illegitimate child, my mother and grandmother stopped speaking regularly. They'd resigned themselves to uncomfortable conversations during holidays and/or birthday phone calls. Until recently. Now they were on the phone all the time and the topic was always me.

One thing I'd noticed about Wyandot County was that there were many, many more churches than there were 7-Elevens. The score was probably something like 15/0. Nana Cole went to Cheswick Community Church, which was north on the 22 just before you got to Big Turtle Point. It was a small, white clapboard church sitting on a slight knoll looking out at Lake Michigan. It was still light out and it would have been worth standing there to take in the view, except the wind had picked up. An unforgiving wind that sounded like the earth screaming.

We parked behind a line of cars on the street, then scurried up the knoll and out behind the church. It was such a small church that they'd put up a very basic building of red corrugated metal with a gray shingled roof behind it. Honestly, I think it was just another pole barn with some upgrades. When you walked in you found yourself in a large windowless space. After a moment, I saw that there were actually a couple of windows, but they were reserved for the offices at the far end.

The big room held three rows of banquet tables. Along the far wall, similar tables had been set up and a bunch of local men in their fifties and sixties were arguing about how to best make pancakes. Seriously, was it that hard? Near the door, there was a heavyset woman sitting behind a card table. Nana Cole smiled and gave her a little wave.

"Dolores, how are you?"

"I'm just fine, Emma. You?"

"Wonderful, just wonderful. This is my grandson, Henry."

I half-smiled. It wasn't that hard to do. Before I left the house, I'd taken a couple of Bev's Valiums. I would have half-smiled at anyone.

"Well hello, Henry. I've heard so much about you."

I wanted to say that most of what she'd heard was probably none of her business, but instead I went from a half-smile to a full smile. What the hey, right?

"My Cheryl Ann is going to be here later. I'll make sure to bring her over."

"How much is it, Dolores?"

"Oh, fifteen dollars each."

I thought fifteen dollars for a plate of pancakes was a bit much. They'd better have all you can eat bacon. Which made me miss my favorite L.A. breakfast place up in Beachwood Canyon. When we were flush, and not too hungover, Vinnie and I would go there on Sundays. Of course, if we were hungover and still horny we went to The French Market—

Nana Cole cleared her throat. "Come along."

The room was half full. People seemed to have divided themselves by age, the largest group being around my nana's age. On the far end of the room there were ten or twelve people in their twenties and early thirties standing loosely together. In between were a few unhappy teenagers and their frazzled parents.

On the edge of the group of twenty-somethings, I noticed a bright orange head. It was the girl who'd been at the sheriff's office with the two middle-aged guys. She was alone, morosely pushing decimated pieces of pancake around her plate.

"There are a few more people I want to introduce you to," Nana Cole said, tucking her arm into mine so I'd have no choice. "I know you don't want to be in Masons Bay forever, but you should get to know a few people. Just for now."

Forever? Who was she kidding? I didn't want to be in Masons Bay next week.

My grandmother proceeded to introduce me to a random collection of senior citizens. None of whom I felt I 'should' know, even if it was 'just for now.' They all seemed to have younger female relatives they wanted to introduce me to sometime. If I were so inclined, I'd have hit the jackpot. Seriously, if I were straight I could be banging a new chick every night. As it was, I had the bad feeling I was going to be stuck dodging invitations for weeks.

Finally, we went over and got pancakes. Unfortunately, there was zero bacon, zero sausage and zero eggs. But, there were chocolate chips, strawberry sauce and whipped cream. There was also enough coffee and sugar cookies to host a Narcotics Anonymous meeting. I got three pancakes and soaked them in strawberry sauce and whipped cream.

"Come over this way," Nana Cole said, leading me back to the old-timers.

"No, I'm going over here."

She gave me a nasty look, like I was abandoning her. Ridiculous. She literally knew every single person there. It wasn't like I was leaving her adrift in a room full of strangers.

I stuck my tongue out at her and she returned the favor. I

wasn't sure what to make of that. Sometimes, I thought I might have liked Nana Cole when she was young. Other times I thought I'd have hated her even more.

I walked over to the other side of the room and sat down next to the girl with orange hair. Her head was perfectly round. That, and the color, reminded me of a billiard ball. I tried to think of the number. I have actually played a lot of pool—mostly at Mother Lode. Of course, I was paying more attention to the guys I played than the game.

I cleared my throat. The girl looked at me and said, "What?" I guess I shouldn't be too surprised she was sitting alone.

"I saw you this morning at the sheriff's office."

"Yeah. I saw you too."

"What's your name? I'm Mooch."

"Mooch? That's stupid. What's your real name?"

"Henry," I said through my gritted teeth. Why did everyone hate my name.

"My name's Opal. What were you doing at the sheriff's office?"

"I had to give a statement. I'm the one who found Sammy Hart."

She stared at me for a moment like maybe I was lying. "I heard Bev Jenkins found him."

"No, it was me. I work for Bev at The Conservancy. There was a note sent there." Of course, now she made me wonder. Had the note been sent to The Conservancy or to Bev? I didn't remember there being a salutation. No 'Dear Bev' at the top.

"You want a medal or something?" Opal asked.

"No. I just, I don't know—I mean, we're just talking"

She leaned over her pancakes and quietly asked, "Why are we just talking? Do you want to screw me?"

"What? *No*." I may have said that a little too emphatically. Embarrassed, I turned to my pancakes and cut out a chunk with my fork. Was everyone up here nuts or was it just this girl?

"Why'd you look at me like that?" she asked.

"Like what?"

"Like I'm a pile of shit somebody's dog left on your lawn. You're not all that you know."

Actually, I was *all that*, but then she'd never been to West Hollywood with me on a Saturday night. She had no clue.

"I wasn't thinking any such thing," I said. "You seem like a very nice girl. I'm sure a lot of guys... wanna screw you."

"You make that sound like an insult."

"You're exhausting, aren't you?"

She scrunched her face at me. "Yeah, I've heard that before."

I ate my pancakes for a while.

"So, is the reward real?"

"Of course, it's real."

"I mean, it's money in a bank account and not just a bunch of promises?"

"Do you know something?"

"Not yet."

"What does that mean?"

"It means not yet." What else would it mean?

"So, what? You're gonna find Sammy's killer so you can get the reward?"

"Yeah, that's the plan," I said. It came out much more lamely than I'd hoped.

Opal put a hand over her face and giggled.

"I'm sorry. Do you think the sheriff is going to catch Sammy's killer?"

That stopped her. "He wouldn't even look for Sammy."

"So, was Sammy like your uncle or something?"

"No. He hung out at the bar I go to in Bellflower. Mr. Chips."

"You mean, like a gay bar?" I asked, lowering my voice.

"Of course, I mean like a gay bar." She rolled her eyes. "A long time ago, Sammy had like a weekly party at his house in Crystal City. He had a mirror ball in his cellar and everything. Then a friend of his wanted to open Mr. Chips and Sammy gave him the money."

I didn't care about any of that. "Exactly when did Sammy disappear?"

"February. Right after Valentine's day."

"How did you know he was gone?"

"There's an HIV clinic connected to Midland Hospital in Bellflower. Sammy was planning a fundraiser for them. Except he didn't show up for a meeting. People started to get worried and we got Rudy Lehmann to go over to the house. Sammy wasn't there."

"Was his house disturbed at all? Did it look like there might have been a fight there?"

"I don't know. They wouldn't let anyone in."

"Then what happened?"

"Nothing. I mean it, nothing. We put up posters, we called *9&10 News*, we started raising money to help find him. Sheriff Crocker didn't do shit."

"Did Sammy have a lot of enemies?"

"He was gay in Wyandot county."

"Is that a yes?"

"Of course it's a yes."

"Is it really that bad here?" I asked. I mean, coming from Los Angeles, well, things weren't always perfect. People got beat up every now and then, but when they did everyone sort of came together and made sure the person was okay.

"Where are you from?"

"L.A."

"Oh God. You wouldn't understand."

I had the feeling she was being super dramatic. "So basically, everyone hated Sammy and would have happily killed him?"

"That isn't what I said."

"Might as well be."

She frowned. "Sammy didn't hide who he was. He was kind of in your face."

"Yeah, I saw the argyle socks," I said dryly.

"I'm not talking about his clothes. It was his behavior. He was a total flamer. I mean, that's what he said about himself so I'm not being an ass. He was light in the loafers and loved it. But this maybe isn't that kind of area. This is more the kind of area where you tone it down."

Said the girl who had orange hair? I didn't think she was toning anything down. Just then Dolores came over and stood at the end of the table with a heavyset girl who had a sweet face and big smile.

"Henry, this is Cheryl Ann."

"Oh, hi—"

"Hi, Opal. How are you?"

"Fine."

Cheryl Ann looked at Opal like she was on the menu; her mother looked at me the same way. Neither of them looked at each other.

"Cheryl Ann. I bet Henry likes movies. The two of you should go to a movie."

"*Chicago* is still at the Orpheum," Cheryl Ann said to Opal.

"I've seen it," Opal replied. I hadn't, but I kept my mouth shut.

"We could go to the multiplex in Bellflower. We could see something else."

"I'm busy," Opal said.

"I didn't say what night."

"Cheryl Ann, why don't you give Henry your number. That way he can call you about the movie."

"555-1867," she said without looking at me.

"Did you get that Henry?" Dolores asked.

"I have a good memory." Yeah, I was going to remember not to call.

"Well, enjoy your pancakes," Dolores said, then pulled Cheryl Ann away.

"Someone has a crush," I said.

Opal gave me dirty look and stood up, saying, "I've had about as much of this as I can take."

At first, I wasn't sure whether she meant talking to me or being at the pancake supper. I mean, it seemed like all she was doing was talking to me, which shouldn't have been too bad. But then I guess she'd been there long enough to know who everyone was and what certain looks meant and what people were probably saying to one another about her talking to me.

Before she walked away, she said, "Look, I want you to know something. I only asked if you wanted to screw me so I could find out if you're gay. I wouldn't have done it."

"So, any guy who doesn't want to screw you is gay?"

"Basically."

Then she walked away. I stared after her. She wasn't like any of the girls I knew in L.A. and I didn't think that was a particularly good thing. I was about to pick up my supper and join my grandmother when a guy of about twenty-five slid into Opal's seat. He was thickly muscled and dark-haired, and would have been cute if not for the angry look on his face.

"You the guy who found Sammy?"

"Yeah, who are you?"

"Rupert Beckett."

"Okay." I struggled to remember the local family trees. Had someone said that Sammy was a Beckett? I kind of thought so, I asked, "Are you related to Sammy?"

"He was my cousin."

"Okay. Did you see him around the time he disappeared?"

He gave me a dirty look. "Why did you find him out there? I mean, is that corner of the Sheck's place, you know, a place where queers go for BJs?"

"In February? I don't think so."

"So then what was he doing out there?"

"I think he was killed somewhere else and brought there."

"That's stupid. I think he went out there to get a BJ and ended up dead."

I almost asked him if he'd ever gotten a BJ outside in the middle of February, but I was afraid he'd tell me a story about getting some poor girl drunk enough to do just that.

"Well, if that's what you think you should maybe tell the sheriff."

He looked at me like I was trying to trick him, and in a way, I was. He was being stupid. I wanted him to do it somewhere else.

"I have to go, my grandmother's waiting." I got up, picking up my plate.

"He deserved what he got," Rupert said. "Don't think he didn't."

Numbly, I walked across the room. What was that about? How could someone say their own relative deserved to be bashed over the head and dumped out in the snow? Could Rupert have killed his cousin? Is that why he was so insistent that Sammy had been cruising in the woods? And if he *had* killed his uncle, how did I prove it?

Nana Cole was finished, so we began to leave. Began, because it took forever. She had to say goodbye to all the people she'd said hello to. We were almost to the door when we stopped to say goodbye to the Reverend Hessel, who was a lumpy looking guy in his late thirties.

"Will we see you on Sunday, Henry?"

"I don't think so."

"We have a service in the evening if you're working. We don't frown on Sunday work like some Christians. People have to do what they have to do."

I felt myself frowning. Why didn't he just let this go?

"I'm not a Christian," I told him while Nana Cole fumed next to me.

"Nonsense. Your grandmother's a Christian and your mother's a Christian. That makes you a Christian."

"Is it a congenital disorder?"

Nana Cole kicked me. It hurt.

"God will be waiting for you when you're ready."

"I hope God has better things to do than wait for me."

"That's not exactly—" I could see him tamp down his anger and decide to turn his other cheek. "I hope you enjoyed your pancakes."

"I did." They were actually very good.

Once we got into the Escalade, Nana Cold asked,

"Did you get that girl's phone number? The one with the orange hair?"

"No. I didn't."

"Just as well. I'm sure you can do better. I'm sure she's nice —it's just, not really a good family. You should probably spend more time with Rupert Beckett. The girls are hanging off him all the time. Maybe he could introduce you to someone nice from a good family."

"I'm not staying here. I want more out of life than living in a backwater town like this."

"Mmm-hmmm. One day at a time."

We didn't say anything else the whole ride home. I really wished she'd figure out that I wasn't going to meet some nice girl and settle down in Wyandot County. It just was *not* going to happen. Seriously, over my dead body.

Chapter 5

ON FRIDAY, I had to examine a yurt. Trust me, until I got to The Conservancy office that morning, I had no idea what that was.

"So, what am I supposed to do?" I asked Bev. She'd just told me, but I didn't really get it.

"Take the camera and get pictures of Sandy Edelson's yurt. We laid out what she was going to build and now we need a record that she's complied."

I looked at her blankly.

"A yurt is like a tent."

"Why do we care if she puts up a tent?"

"It's like a permanent tent."

"Oh." I tried to make sense of that. A permanent tent would be like a building, except with canvas walls. And a canvas ceiling.

"Go and take pictures, okay? I've got to go to the ladies' room. Too much coffee."

She zipped out of the room to the tiny lavatory in the back. The Wyandot Land Conservancy office was an itty-bitty room in the back of what had once been a hundred-year-old house which was now carved into three businesses: a hairdresser, a bookstore and The Conservancy. We shared the lavatory with the hairdresser.

The second Bev was gone, I took her purse out from under the desk and looked through it. The first prescription bottle I picked up was Dilantin. I wasn't sure what that was for, but I was pretty sure it wasn't a fun drug. I dug around some more and found the diazepam. She only had four pills left. That was a problem. She had to know she only had four pills, so I couldn't take any. Shit. The last time I'd visited Bev's purse—which had only been two weeks before—she'd had twenty or thirty pills. Obviously, she had some kind of medical problem. I mean, first of all, Dilantin, and second of all, she was taking a lot more Valium than I was.

Putting her purse back under the desk, I wondered what to do. I'd taken the last Valium the day before while I was watching DVDs on my iBook and hanging out with Reilly. I'd gone to Hometown Video and rented *Body of Evidence*. I wanted to watch something that might help me figure out how to investigate a murder and that was the best option they had. Of course, it hadn't turned out to be particularly helpful.

Oh, and before I continue: My iBook G3 was fabulous. I'd gotten one of the last lime green Mac clamshells with a DVD player. It cost me a fortune and I was desperately hoping the credit card I'd used wouldn't track me down since I basically hadn't paid for it two years later. It was worth the suspense though. I adored the laptop and felt like I'd die without it. Okay, I probably wouldn't die, but a short coma was a definite possibility.

Bev came back from the bathroom. "You're still here?"

"Sorry, I thought there was more."

"No. Get going."

I had the address and the map of the parcel, so I went out to the F-150 and studied my gas station map. At that point I had no idea if Sandy Edelson was a boy Sandy or a girl Sandy. Whoever Sandy turned out to be they lived just off Big Turtle Highway on Laverne Road. It was going to take nearly half an hour to get there. The F-150 did not have a CD player or even a cassette deck. If not for my iPod I'd have had to listen to the radio. Ugh. I popped in my earbuds and listened to an ancient

Elliot Smith album I'd loved when I was like seventeen—I was a very depressed seventeen.

When I finally got out to Sandy Edelson's I was sure I was lost—and a little sad from the music. I put my iPod away and checked the address again. It matched. But it shouldn't. I was staring at a single-wide trailer, which didn't make sense. Most of the places I visited were farms or one time a vacation home. And yet, here I was.

Taking out my flip phone I called The Conservancy, but there was no answer. I was going to have to go up to the trailer and embarrass myself.

It was one of those older ones from the late fifties or early sixties—back when cars had fins—red on the top and bottom and white in the middle. The paint job was recent so it looked, well, kind of cute. There was a little white picket fence on one side that defined a garden. Tiny white flowers had already bloomed—which was weird since there was still snow on the ground.

I climbed the little stoop and knocked on the door. There were flower boxes on the windows, obviously Sandy was planning to grow some flowers or herbs. From the look of the boxes —the soil had been turned—he or she was chomping at the bit to plant seeds.

The door was abruptly opened by a woman of around thirty, I guessed. She was thin, brunette, and dressed in a snug pair of jeans and an obviously homemade knit, purple-and-mustard poncho—I was fairly certain it was a first project. The bottom edge was much more consistent than the top edge.

"I'm looking for Sandy Edelson?" I said, with a questioning tone.

"That's me."

"Oh, great. I'm Henry Milch from The Wyandot Land Conservancy."

"Bev sent you!"

"Yes, she did. I need to take some photos of your yurt."

"No problem. Let me get my boots."

"Um, I wonder, could I use your bathroom?" I asked, managing to blush a little.

"Of course, come on in."

She held the storm door open for me and I stepped inside. The living room was small, furnished with second-hand pieces from the fifties—seriously, it was right out of an episode of *I Love Lucy*. The walls were covered in wood veneer. She pointed me through the kitchen, but as I started, she said, "Could you take your boots off, please?"

"Oh, yeah, sure." Fortunately, I'd gotten the kind with a zipper on the front, so I was able to step out of them pretty quick. I walked through the kitchen with its mini-appliances and turquoise Formica, and then I turned into the bathroom. It was a cramped little room with lime green tile. I shut the door behind me and, as quietly as possible, opened her medicine cabinet.

What a disappointment: vitamins, Saint-John's-wort, a bunch of little brown bottles with droppers, Band-Aids, echinacea, iron pills, more Band-Aids, cotton balls, natural toothpaste, Scope mouthwash. I couldn't believe it. Almost everyone had a little something lying around. Didn't this woman ever have dental work? Didn't she ever get sad or anxious or depressed?

Her medicine cabinet was almost as bad as Nana Cole's. I'd scoped that out the night I arrived. She didn't have anything good either, just high blood pressure medicine and baby aspirin. Sandy didn't even have aspirin. It was absurd.

After flushing the toilet, I went back out to the living room. While I was gone, rather than put on a coat which might have been appropriate since it was cloudy and in the forties, she'd added a ridiculous scarf around her neck and a matching pair of gloves. I was wrong; she hadn't learned anything about kitting from making the poncho.

"Do you live here alone?" I asked, as I put my boots on. I mean, after looking through her medicine cabinet I figured she did, but it was polite to ask.

"I do," she said, as we walked out. "I used to come up here

on vacation from Detroit, and I just loved it. Then I found this place. It was surprisingly affordable since it's under easement."

"Twenty-five acres?"

"That's right. This is the only corner that's perkable. So I was thinking of building a house here, but then I just kind of fell in love with my little trailer. So I've been fixing—"

"What's perkable?"

"Suitable for a septic system."

"Oh, I see." This was my life now. Talking to strangers about sewage. I had to find a way to go home.

"Of course there's all sorts of other rules about where I can build and stuff—but you know all that."

I would if I'd read the easement, but I hadn't done that.

"The yurt is just up this road," she said, leading me over to a dirt road that led up a steep hill. "Bev said you're from California."

"I am. Born and raised."

"I've been out there. It's nice, but I think I'd miss the seasons."

There was still snow on the hill we'd begun to climb, though the road was dry. My boots suddenly seemed very heavy. It was hard to breathe so I just let Sandy talk.

"I teach personal enrichment classes. They're a combination of nutrition, yoga, breathing, spiritual centering and self-applied acupressure."

"Uh-huh," I said. No matter how hard she tried, she'd never make anyone feel as good two Vicodin and a strawberry margarita.

"I heard you had some trouble the other day."

"Oh. Not trouble... not exactly. Just... you know, a dead body."

She nodded, "Sammy Hart."

How did word get around so fast? Was there a message board I wasn't on? As though reading my mind, she said, "I was in Drip, the coffee place in Bellflower, and I heard people talking about it. They weren't talking to me, mind you. I've only been here a couple of years. A lot of the old families still treat me like I'm a fudgie."

We'd reached the top of the hill and I began trying to calm my breath.

"It's just down this path."

"Did you just put this in?" I asked.

"Oh no, I put it in last fall. Bev thought it made more sense to wait until spring for the photos."

"I see."

"The pictures are really just a formality," she said. "For the file. But you know that. Why am I telling you?"

She led me down a path about twenty feet. There was a dark blue, round tent that looked like it might have fit in well at King Arthur's court. Set into the tent was a metal door.

"Wow, it looks really permanent. I mean, for a tent."

"There are four separate layers of cloth over a metal frame. It's really very nice," she said, opening the door. I walked in.

Inside, it was a large, round space with a smooth wood floor.

"I'm planning to transfer my classes here. There's a composting toilet outside."

I wondered if she had to meet certain requirements to run a business out of her yurt, but decided not to open that can of worms, particularly when she asked, "Did you know him? Sammy Hart, I mean."

"No. I've only been here about six weeks. From what I understand he disappeared around the time I got here." She must have known that though so why—I asked, "Did *you* know him?"

"I did. He was one of my students. He was making a lot of progress on his journey and then, right before he disappeared, something happened. It was like his aura completely changed."

I didn't know what that meant, but it sounded painful. Then I realized I'd just stumbled onto my first witness. Sandy might know something. Something I might be able to turn into reward money. I asked, "And you have no idea what was, um, bothering him?"

"No," she said, though she seemed doubtful. "I mean... as I said, I haven't started teaching here yet. I still teach at a studio in Hemmet."

"Okay," I didn't know why she'd changed directions. I had the sinking feeling she wouldn't tell me anything useful. "Where's Hemmet again?"

"It's on the way to Bellflower. Easy to miss. The studio is in Lila Langley's basement. Hence the yurt. It's going to be so much better. Anyway, I have to clean up after class, so I leave five or ten minutes after my students. This one day, I think it was right around Valentine's, I came out and Sammy's still there. Standing by his giant SUV talking to this woman very intently."

This was much better. "Do you remember what she looked like?"

"Dark. Very dark."

"Hair? Skin? Clothes?"

"Aura."

I was afraid of that. Not a description I could give to Detective Lehmann.

"It was nearly black. I know that sounds like someone truly evil, but it doesn't necessarily mean that. It can just mean that someone's upset or they're experiencing a nervous disruption. I mean, it can also indicate disease, but that's usually localized. And I remember seeing nothing but black."

"I see," I said, because I didn't.

"I got the impression she'd been driving along—"

"The woman with the black aura."

"Yes. Her car was parked at an angle as though she'd parked suddenly, carelessly. She must have seen Sammy, pulled over, and jumped out of the car."

"Do you know what kind of car it was?"

"Red?"

"You don't sound sure."

"Maybe brown."

She saw auras but not the color of cars.

"So, the woman with the black aura. Was she young, old? Was her hair dark too? How tall was she?"

"Oh gosh. Her hair was light brown and she was shorter than Sammy but still tall. I'd guess she'd be a little younger than I am."

"So, like, uh, what exactly happened?"

"I really shouldn't be gossiping like this," she said, biting her lip. "It's just, well, he's dead and I have to tell someone what I saw."

"Uh-huh," I had the feeling that if I just waited she'd tell—

"The thing is she yelled at Sammy for a while. Sammy remained calm, although his aura also became agitated. It was like this cloud descended on them both."

"How did it end?"

"I was thinking of going over and trying to calm them down, but the woman said something, something which must have been very insulting because Sammy took a step back, and then she rushed to her car. He got into his SUV before I got there so I didn't talk to him. I never saw him again."

"Okay, well, great. I guess I should go then."

"Um," she said. "Aren't you here to take photos?"

"Oh. Yeah."

Chapter 6

I SPENT the rest of the day playing *Warcraft III*. It was frustrating because the DSL was not great. I mean, I know I was lucky to have it at all. The phone company had just started offering it, and there was a phone line in my room from when my teenage mom had spent hours and hours on her princess phone. Still, it just happened to go down every time I joined a campaign, so it wasn't just annoying for me, it was annoying for others.

My mother called again. A couple of times. I didn't answer my cell. After the last time, the phone rang downstairs a minute later and I knew she was talking to Nana Cole. When I first arrived, my grandmother would have come up the stairs and tried to get me to come to the phone. That had gone badly a few times so now she didn't bother.

I was edgy as I waited for their phone call to end. Finally, I heard Nana Cole turn on *Star Search*, which she loved even though she hated Arsenio Hall and didn't understand why they couldn't bring back Ed McMahon. I snuck into the bathroom and took a shower as quietly as I could—I had a plan, one that I didn't want to discuss with my grandmother—and a shower after dinner would tip her off.

Honestly, I was so excited and all I was planning was a trip to this presumably pathetic gay bar, Mr. Chips. There was no way it would compare to a West Hollywood bar, but on the upside, it was not twenty-five hundred miles away.

After my shower, which I had apparently gotten away with, I took my time getting ready. I had a pair of faded jeans that was ripped in all the right places—they were perfect. I still couldn't believe that Nana Cole had tried to throw them out twice. She had absolutely no fashion sense. With it, I wanted to wear a T-shirt I'd gotten on Melrose, which was purple with black sequins spread around the shoulders and chest. The problem was it was still freezing out at night—and also in the daytime—so I'd have to wear a coat or at least a sweater, which meant no one would see the shirt. I mean, what did people do with winter coats in a gay bar? I'd never been to a gay bar in a place where people wore coats. Actually, I was used to boys wearing as little as possible.

Finally, I decided I had no choice but to wear the old Irish sweater that had been my grandfather's. Nana Cole had given it to me: my inheritance. I could leave my puffer jacket in the truck and run into the bar.

Of course, I couldn't wear the boots she'd bought me. They were gigantic and made me feel like Frankenstein's monster. Instead, I decided to wear my black Kenneth Cole loafers, the ones with the square toe. They were years out-of-date—something I didn't think anyone here would notice—so it wouldn't be a tragedy if I ruined them running back and forth from the truck to the bar.

I was completely ready before nine, which was not going to work. If I was going to go to Mr. Chips I was definitely not showing up before ten. Even that was early. It only took twenty-five minutes to get to Bellflower so I had to wait. I couldn't go downstairs and watch TV with Nana Cole, she'd want to know where I was going. Besides, I knew that later on she'd drift off watching *Hannity & Colmes* so I could slip out then.

I flipped open my iBook and navigated to AppleWorks. I decided I should think through what I'd learned about Sammy Hart. At first, I stared at a blank screen. Had I actually learned anything? I knew he was gay. I knew that he didn't die where I'd found him. I knew the killer might have had an accomplice to help carry the body. I knew that his family hated him. I knew that he had a confrontation with a dark-aura-ed woman shortly before he disappeared. And I knew that none of that was enough to get me the reward money.

What did I need to find out? Maybe that was a better thing to be typing onto the blank page. What did I need? I needed... a confession. So that meant I was doing the right thing, talking to people. But how was I going to get someone to confess to me? I mean, evidence would work too, but I didn't even know what Sammy had been killed with. A blow to the head, that's all I knew.

I could hardly start collecting random things that would kill a person if you used it to bash them on the head. That's a super large collection. Now, if I knew *where* Sammy was killed. Wait, the last time he was seen he was... actually, all I knew was the first time he was missed. He was supposed to be at a meeting right after Valentine's Day and didn't show. He was wearing argyle socks. *Was that typical meeting attire for him?* I wondered. Was he on his way to the meeting and he got waylaid? And, where was his car? That was something important I needed to find out. It was nearly ten and I hadn't typed a single word into my iBook.

Oh well. Time to go.

Just as I'd thought, Nana Cole was fast asleep in her favorite chair. Walking through the room I could tell the program was awful. It was the political equivalent of Saturday morning wrestling: Everyone had a part to play, no one ever got terribly hurt, and the winners were decided beforehand. The fact that Nana Cole thought Hannity walked on water didn't make the program any more realistic.

Quick as a flash, I was out of the house and into the truck. I started it up and drove halfway down the long driveway before I turned the lights on. Since I'd mostly driven to Bellflower in the daytime, driving there at night was a little nerve-wracking since I wasn't quite sure where I was in the dark. *And* it was dark. Very, very dark.

It still surprised me how much darker it was in Michigan than it was in L.A. And by much darker I mean pitch black. Of course, there were other nights, nights when there was a full moon and it seemed like it was practically daytime. The lights in L.A. kept it from getting truly dark; they also kept it from getting lit up by a full moon.

I took 22 the whole way to Bellflower since I was least likely to get lost that way. I think there might have been a faster way, but I didn't know it yet. And driving around the backroads to save a few minutes wasn't such a great idea. Cannibal movies, remember?

Bellflower had two whole thriving streets of shops and entertainment. They went on for maybe four blocks and then petered out. On one of the side streets between Lakeside and First, I still couldn't remember which one, Mr. Chips was squeezed between an antique shop and a place that sold pasties. Pasties are this kind of pie you could pick up and eat, not stripper wear as I'd first thought.

Outside, the bar wasn't too much more than a window with a beer sign and a door—not promising at all. On the door, rather discretely I thought, was a rainbow flag sticker with a smiley face in the middle. I think the smiley face was meant to throw people off.

Inside, it was a very old-timey place. It could have come straight out of the fifties or sixties. Actually, since I wasn't alive in the fifties or sixties, what I mean is that it looked just like the bars I've seen in old movies and TV shows. There was a long bar with stools on one side of the skinny room, and a line of vinyl booths on the other. Where the bar ended, there was an open space with an electrified dartboard. There was a jukebox over there too. Some Eminem song was playing, total straight boy music. Seriously, where was I?

Above the bar, a TV was playing. In L.A. I would have expected Kylie and Britney music videos; but here it was the late news. Apparently, we had just snatched control of the airport in Baghdad. Hey, maybe they were right and we'd be out of there in a couple of months—not that we should have been there in the first place.

If the bar was from the sixties, the patrons were full-on '90s grunge band. Lots and lots of flannel. I mean, it was cold out, but there are other ways to keep warm. Putting aside my reservations, I went up to the bar and ordered an Absolut appletini.

"Do you want that on the rocks?"

"God no," I said. Sacrilege, he might as well have asked if I wanted Cheez Whiz on a communion wafer.

While I waited for the drink, I looked around the room. I was looking for an orange head of hair. I didn't see it. I also didn't see a lot of attractive people. To me, it didn't even look like a gay bar. It looked more like the bar where every weirdo from high school would come when they were old enough to drink. And if that were true, there wouldn't be a whole lot of room for actual gays.

Over in a booth, I saw the two English teachers I'd noticed at the sheriff's office with someone whose hair was purple. I squinted and saw that it was Opal.

I paid only four dollars for my drink, which was very cheap by L.A. standards and would have been fabulous if the drink wasn't terrible. After my first sip, I was certain they'd only ever bought one bottle of Absolut and had been refilling it with dollar-store vodka ever since. I left a two-dollar tip hoping the bartender would like me enough to use an actual top-shelf vodka when I came back.

I walked over to the booth where the English teachers sat with the now purple-headed Opal.

"You changed your hair," I said.

"I was depressed."

"They have pills for that."

"I'm not hurting anybody."

I shrugged. I did think she might be hurting her hair. She turned to the English teachers and said, "This is Henry."

"Mooch," I corrected.

One of them said, "Nice to meet you, Henry. I'm Phil and this is Richard."

Upon closer inspection, I saw that Phil was much younger than Richard, around forty. Better looking too, with most of his own hair. Richard though was in his late fifties and looked every day of it. He had dark circles under his eyes and even in bar light looked kind of green.

"Hey," I said.

"Do you want to join us?"

"Well, I was kind of waiting for Brad Pitt to walk in, but obviously he's stood me up—again! —so, um, sure."

None of them laughed at my joke. I mean, I knew their friend had just died but, seriously, it was funny. Once I was in the booth, pushed up against Opal, I noticed there was a stack of the reward announcements sitting there. They were giving them out. Which did not make me happy. The last thing in the world I needed was competition.

Opal must have seen where I was looking because she said, "Henry thinks he's going to find Sammy's killer and get the reward."

She probably rolled her eyes, though since she was next to me it was hard to tell.

"Opal, don't be mean," Phil said. "The whole point of offering the reward was that *someone, anyone,* would try to find Sammy's killer. Don't pull an attitude just because he's willing to try."

"He has no experience."

"The sheriff has experience. How much do you think he's doing?"

"Well, have you caught the killer yet?" Opal asked me. I was beginning to get the impression she and I weren't going to be friends.

"It's been like two days."

"So what have you done? Besides watching *Law & Order* for pointers."

That was uncomfortably close to the truth. I decided to turn this around. I mean, no matter what I said I didn't think Opal was going to suddenly be nice. "What is it you do?"

"I'm in retail. But I'm studying to be a therapist." That

sounded like a terrible idea since her solution to depression was purple hair.

I turned to Phil and Richard. Richard said, "I'm a librarian at the Bellflower District Library."

"I own Village Books," Phil said.

"People up here read a lot," I observed.

"The winters are long."

"So—change of subject," I said, wanting to find out something more important than the local literacy rate. "When Sammy disappeared where was his car?"

"It was in his driveway," Richard said.

Which led me to immediately say, "I think there's a strong possibility he was killed at his home."

"What? Are you psychic?" Opal asked.

"No, I'm *not* psychic. When I found his body, he had on a nice pair of loafers—"

"He was always so particular about his shoes," Phil said.

"Anyway, he wouldn't have walked out there in the snow, not in those shoes. That means he was probably killed somewhere else. And since his car was in his own driveway then it's very likely he was killed at home and then his body was dumped out at the Sheck's place."

"Someone might have picked him up. You know, given him a ride," Opal suggested, but I didn't think she was really committed to it. She just wanted to be contrary.

"He was going to a meeting, right? That's what he was dressed for. Do you *know* that someone was bringing him to that meeting?"

They looked at each other, then shook their heads.

"We have to get into his house."

"That's not—" Richard started but was cut off.

"No problem," Phil said. "I have a key."

"You—? Why do you have a key?" Richard wanted to know.

"In case of emergency."

"So, why didn't you go in before?" I asked. "While he was missing?"

"The detective said not to," Phil explained. "He said it was against the law. I didn't want to get arrested."

Something was off. Why did Lehmann do that? It certainly didn't fit with my understanding of TV detective shows. Gil Grissom would never tell someone that—oh wait, he wasn't actually a detective. *CSI* is probably not that helpful.

Just then, a slouchy young man walked by the booth and snagged a flyer for the reward. I wanted to jump up and break his arm. Or at least give him a tongue-lashing.

Opal glared at Phil. "I would have gone in if I'd known you had a key. I would have gone in."

"Which is why I didn't say anything about the key. I didn't want *anyone* getting arrested."

"Why now?" I asked. "Why is it okay now?"

"They've released the house."

"How do you know that?" Richard wanted to know.

"I'm the executor on his will."

"Oh *really*?" I said, sipping my awful appletini. "Tell us then, what's in the will?"

"Yes, Phil, tell us what's in it!" Richard said, a sudden edge in his voice.

"Well, Roger Linkletter gets Sammy's share of the bar." Opal nodded as though that seemed fair and expected. Richard's face remained sour. Phil continued, "And, uh, I get the house."

Richard slowly closed his eyes. His upper lip quivered. Phil watched him closely but went on as calmly as possible.

"Then there's some money for local charities. The Turly HIV Clinic, of course, and the LGBT hotline. And a bequest to the Human Rights Campaign."

Taking a deep breath, Richard asked, "He didn't leave me anything? Not a penny?"

"I'm sorry, Richard," Phil said. "If you need—"

"It's not about the money."

I was old enough to know that when people said 'It's not about the money' it almost always was.

"I think it's great that Roger keeps the bar," Opal said, diplomatically. "Mr. Chips really matters to a lot of people."

"There's more," Phil said. "There's a very large piece of property that's been left to The Wyandot Land Conservancy."

That was odd. Not the donation. I mean, it was odd that we'd gotten the note that led to the discovery of his body and now The Conservancy was inheriting—was there a connection?

"Well, I for one need another drink," Richard said, getting up out of the booth. He looked at Phil and said, "Fine, I'll get this round." Then to me he asked, "What is that monstrosity?"

"The world's worst appletini. I'll have a Ketel One and tonic. And please make sure there's actual Ketel One in the bottle."

They were staring at me. "What? I ordered Absolut but it was obviously well vodka. No one in L.A. would try to get away with that."

Richard slunk over to the bar. Opal leaned over and said, "I didn't want to say this in front of Richard—I think he had a thing for Sammy—but Sammy was seeing someone new before he died. He told me."

"Did he?" Phil said. "Why would he tell you?"

"Why wouldn't he tell me? We were friends."

"Of course, you were friends. I didn't say you weren't. I just didn't know you were *that* kind of friend."

"Well, he didn't tell me who he was seeing, but then he liked to be mysterious."

"Yes, he did, didn't he?"

"I'd like to look at Sammy's house," I said to Phil. "When can I see it?"

Richard came back to the table empty-handed. "Sorry kids, my credit card was declined. I'm sure it's just bookkeeping, I sent the payment in."

Phil stood up. "I'll get us a drink then." Before he walked over to the bar, he said to me, "Come into the bookstore around two-ish. We'll leave from there."

Then he walked away. Richard followed.

Due to my probably blank look, Opal asked, "What?"

"I thought he was the librarian."

"No, Richard is the librarian. Phil owns the bookstore in Masons Bay."

"Oh. I live right outside of Masons Bay."

"How nice. You know where you live."

Glaring at her for a moment, I got up and wandered off to find someone to buy me drinks for the rest of the night. And *that* is the last thing I remember.

Chapter 7

"COME ON, wake up. I have to go to work."

I struggled to open my eyes. Blinking a few times, I realized I was on a mattress laid directly on the floor of a very small, windowless room. *My God, have I been kidnapped?* I shut my eyes hoping the next time I opened them I'd be somewhere else.

"I'm serious. I do *really* have to go to work."

Someone was shaking me, tugging me. I pried open an eye. The man shaking me was in his thirties, had done a very bad job shaving, and wore a name tag pinned onto his light blue shirt: BILL TOUHY, MANAGER. I vaguely remembered him.

"How'd you get a name like Henry?" He'd asked after he bought me a Ketel One and tonic.

"My mother used to tell me it was because of the kid in *E.T.* She thought he was cute, but then I figured out I was two years old when the movie came out. She finally explained that she'd had a crush on her tenth grade English teacher and his name was Henry."

It was a story I'd told before. Like many of my mother's stories it was completely untrue.

"You were born when your mom was in high school?"

"No. She just… it was a memorable crush."

"I like the first story better. Can I pretend you're the kid from *E.T.*?"

"That's disgusting."

Bill Touhy, Manager, pulled me into a sitting position and said, "You need to get dressed. I have to drive you back to your car."

"Truck. I have a truck."

"Okay. Whatever."

Well, it seemed important. I didn't want to be dropped off in front of some random car. Bill Touhy, Manager, was collecting my clothes and dumping them next to me. Slowly, I pulled on my sweater, my grandfather's sweater. I wondered how my grandfather's sweater ended up in a strange man's bedroom.

I was still high. I could figure that much out. I'd been there enough times. And honestly, it was very pleasant. Cozy, comfy, sleepy. And would have been more so if Bill Touhy, Manager, would let me go back to sleep.

Except he wouldn't.

My sweater was on. I'd done it myself. Mostly. Bill Touhy, Manager, pulled me to my feet. My choices were pull on my jeans or stand there naked from the waist down. I reached for my jeans.

"Please hurry. I'm supposed to be there by ten and if I'm late it sets a bad example."

"Uh-huh."

I had another little memory from the night before. I'd asked Bill Touhy, Manager, if he knew where I could get some Oxy. And he said he still had some leftover from when he had dental surgery. Things were getting a bit clearer.

He buttoned my jeans for me and put on my socks. I think he'd completely given up the idea of my doing it myself. He slipped on my shoes and shoved my jacket at me. Then he pushed me through his bedroom door. We were in a basement —which explained the windowless kidnap room. To our left was a sliding glass door and we headed for that. When we got outside, I saw a wide, muddy driveway, a sagging wooden garage, a house built on a mound above us, and a lot of pine trees.

"Where am I?"

"Crystal Lake."

I had no idea where that was, so I didn't know if it mattered.

"I work in Bellflower so it's not a problem taking you back to your car," Bill Touhy, Manager, said as though it mattered.

We said almost nothing on the thirty-five-minute ride. Okay, I might have fallen back to sleep. Right before we got to Bellflower my phone rang. It was Nana Cole. I didn't answer. She must be pretty worried if she's calling my cell phone.

I checked to see if I had any voicemails and I did. Nana Cole had called before. Twice. My mother had called. Once. I didn't listen to the messages. I mean, seriously, why bother.

The truck was a few doors down from Mr. Chips. Bill Touhy, Manager, pulled up next to it.

"Well, it was very nice to meet you."

"Oh yeah, me too."

"Um, are you going to be okay to drive?"

"Sure," I said. I didn't have much choice.

"You probably shouldn't have taken as many pills as you did."

"Really?" I said, acid in my voice. "That would never have occurred to me."

"Sorry. Just take a short nap if you need to."

It was like thirty-some degrees out. I'd get hypothermia. But I said, "I will, thanks."

I got out and he drove off. I have to say, I was relieved there was no final kiss or exchange of numbers or a promise to do it again sometime. In L.A., Bill Touhy, Manager, would have been what Vinnie called 'three-drinks pretty,' meaning that after three-drinks he got a lot more attractive. It was morning, though, and I was sober. Or, sober-ish. Whatever appeal he'd had the night before was gone.

Climbing into my truck I had the terrible realization that I'd just had sex for drugs. As soon I thought that, I decided I was wrong. I had *not* just had sex for drugs. It was true that Bill Touhy, Manager, was not up to my L.A. standard—I almost never settled for 'three-drinks pretty'—but it had been a while, a long while, and I was desperate. *And*, this was Wyandot County so pickings were slim. That's why I'd had sex with him. The fact that he gave me some leftover Oxy was coincidental.

I mean, if you have sex with a guy and he gives you a glass of water are you exchanging sex for water? Of course not. Just because two things happen one after the other does not mean they're connected. I did not have sex for drugs. I did not have sex for drugs. I did not have sex for drugs. I repeated that the whole drive from Bellflower to Masons Bay.

As I pulled into Nana Cole's driveway, I was feeling good. The alcohol had definitely worn off and there was still enough Oxy in my system to keep me from having a hangover. I was also a tad more awake.

I parked and got out of the truck. I whistled for Reilly. He came running and jumped on me a few times, covering me in mud. Again. Thank God Nana Cole did my laundry.

I could see her on the other side of the yard picking up the dead branches that had blown off the trees during the winter. She was making a pile in the fire ring. I remembered the fire ring from childhood visits. It was a big deal in the summer. I remembered toasting marshmallows when I was ten.

I walked up to her and said, "I saw that you called. I was driving so I didn't want to pick up."

She walked over to me and said, "You smell like liquor."

"Because I was drinking. That's why I didn't drive home last night. I didn't want to get arrested."

There was an awkward moment while I waited to see if she'd buy it. I couldn't keep waiting though, so I added the lie, "I was being responsible."

"Where did you stay?"

"With that girl, Opal. Her hair's purple now."

"I thought you didn't take her number?"

"Oh, she found me on Friendster." Also untrue.

"I don't know what that means," Nana Cole said.

"The computer."

She gave me a grumpy look and said, "Feed your dog."

Reilly and I walked back to the house and I wondered when he became *my* dog?

———

EVEN THOUGH VILLAGE BOOKS was right on the other side of The Conservancy, I'd never actually been inside. I parked in front, rather than in the back like I usually did, and walked up to what had once been a side porch. The building was a large single-family house that had been painted emerald green with bright white trim.

The bookstore was divided into four small rooms, which I believe had once been parts of larger rooms. Books were everywhere, in bookcases, baskets, shelving attached to the walls, stacked on chairs and even on the floor. There was a bulletin board next to the door. Among the notices was the flyer about the reward. I was tempted to rip it down and put it in my pocket.

I couldn't though because Phil was standing right there behind the counter next to a display for the book *The Lovely Bones.* He was talking to a tall man in his mid-thirties. The man was good-looking with hair the color of straw and a prominent Adam's apple—which could have detracted from his attractiveness but somehow didn't.

I thought I'd busy myself poking around while they talked, but Phil held up a finger to stop the man—who was gossiping about someone who was about to lose his job—and said, "Henry, this is Toddy Milner. He runs the Turley HIV Clinic. We're fairly certain he's the last person to talk to Sammy."

"Really? You talked to him on the day he disappeared?"

"It's nice to meet you too," he said, with a pleasant snarl.

"Oh, I'm sorry. Yeah, it's nice to meet you."

He smiled. "Sammy was supposed to attend a meeting for the fundraiser we were working on. The time had changed, so I called him around ten that morning to tell him."

"Uh-huh. What time was the meeting?"

"At three."

"But he didn't show up?"

"No."

"So he must have been killed sometime between ten and three."

"That I wouldn't know. I suppose it's plausible."

"Was he HIV positive?" I asked.

Toddy put his hands up like I was robbing him. "I can't answer that. I can't discuss anyone's medical information."

"What if that's why he was killed though?"

"I can respond to a warrant, but I haven't gotten one yet."

"So the sheriff hasn't asked you that question?"

"I don't know that they'd need to. The autopsy would tell them most of what they need to know about Sammy's health."

"Oh, yeah, I guess that's true."

What else did I want to know? This guy was obviously important so I shouldn't screw up this opportunity.

"Is it true that Sammy ran a disco out of his basement?" I asked. "Did you go there?"

Toddy gasped. "I'm much too young for that! We're talking about the seventies. I was a toddler. I was hardly venturing out to makeshift discos."

I glanced at Phil.

"Before my time too. If we're talking the late seventies I might have been old enough but not out of the closet. I didn't think there were any gays up here. People acted like it was something that only happened in the city. Why do you ask?"

I shrugged. *Why had I asked?*

"I don't know. It just seems kind of weird."

And it did seem weird. I mean, I came out in high school. Well, to my mother and some friends, but still it didn't seem possible that someone would have had to hide a disco in their basement. Like, was that the way guys met then? Probably just in places like Wyandot County. They had gay bars in cities. They've always had gay bars in cities, right?

"We've lost so much," Phil said. At first, I thought he meant Sammy, but he continued, "Our history has been slipping away for decades. We lose a little bit more with each death."

Toddy added, "I tried to get Sammy to write something down about those times, but he didn't like to think about it all."

I had the feeling there was more to that story, but I didn't get to pursue it because Toddy asked, "Now, where did *you* come from? You seem to have popped up out of nowhere."

"I live with my grandmother, Emma Cole. I used to live in L.A."

"Why would you ever leave?"

"Money problems," I said. Not the truth, but much easier to explain.

"Well, I'm sure you'll get back on your feet," Toddy said, tapping me on the shoulder. "Pretty boys like you always do."

That left me blushing—even though I completely agreed.

He looked over at Phil, saying, "I have to run, see you later."

Toddy walked out of the bookstore. Phil said, "Let me just get my coat and we can go."

He put on a thin raincoat even though I still wore my winter coat. I mean, it was in the forties, it seemed more appropriate. Before we left the bookstore, he picked up a cardboard sign which was half paper clock. It said, I'LL BE BACK AT… on the top and then you'd set the clock's time. He set it for a full hour later.

"Are you sure you can leave for so long?" I asked. "We could probably do this later."

"Don't worry about it. People are used to me popping in and out. If anyone comes, they'll come back."

We decided he would drive and we climbed into a beat-up Subaru sitting at the curb. Believe it or not, the backseat was full of books. When he started the car, the CD player came on. Frank Sinatra wanting to fly to the moon. I was going to have to struggle to stay awake.

"So, Toddy runs the HIV clinic. Does that mean a lot of people up here have AIDS?"

"It's not really the number that's important. It's that people with HIV in rural places like Wyandot County are more likely to have trouble accessing healthcare and more likely to suffer stigma. It's not unusual up here for people to come to get tested only to find out they've already got AIDS."

He was talking to me as though I understood HIV in the

big city. Honestly, I didn't know that much about it. I went to The Center to get tested about every six months—okay, once a year—and I used to go to fundraisers whenever I could get comped, but that was really the extent of my knowledge. I mean, I knew it was still out there and that it affected people. It just never affected anyone I knew.

Phil continued, "A lot of what the Turley Clinic does is prevention. You know, needle exchange, condom distribution, safe sex pamphlets, things like that."

He kept on talking about the clinic for the rest of the ride to Bellflower. I didn't even have to ask questions. It was like he'd memorized everything ever written about the place and wanted to get rid of it by telling me.

We finally pulled up in front of Sammy Hart's house. It was what they call a Painted Lady: A Victorian house painted in at least three separate colors. Don't get too excited, I really don't know anything about architecture. I went out with this guy when I was at UCLA whose idea of a date was to take me to a particularly un-trendy part of L.A. and look at old houses. The best part of that day was finding the house they showed at the beginning of *Charmed*. I *love* that show. When I die I want to come back as a witch. Or a warlock. Or whatever.

Sammy's house was in a neighborhood full of big old houses with porches and turrets and wide lawns. It was two blocks from the commercial area where I'd been the night before. A shiny, silver Land Rover sat in the driveway. I wasn't sure, but I thought they were super expensive. Did someone kill Sammy for his money? It was a nice house. A really nice house. Maybe Phil killed him to get it? Especially if it came with that car. Of course, if he were the killer he probably wouldn't have volunteered to show me the house. Right?

As we got out of the car, Phil took a deep breath and said, "It was me."

Chapter 8

OF COURSE, the minute he said that I jumped inside. A confession! Perfect! All I had to do was turn Phil in and collect the reward. And maybe avoid going into the house with him. That no longer seemed like such a good idea. Yup, everything was going be just fine. I could almost feel the California sun on my skin.

Unfortunately, he continued, "Opal told you Sammy was seeing someone. It was me. He wanted to keep things on the down low because of Richard. I thought it was silly though, I mean we're all grownups for God's sake."

To avoid letting him see the disappointment on my face, I said, "Can we go inside? It's kind of cold out here."

"Oh sure," he said, holding up his keys. "Let's go."

We walked up the porch and stopped at the front door. I noticed that his key to the house was on his keychain and not on a separate ring. Did that mean he used it a lot? If he was the one seeing Sammy, he probably did. He opened the door and we walked into a large foyer with a well-polished wooden table in the center. There were doors on either side and a stairway to the upper two floors.

"The furnace is set to fifty," Phil explained. "If you think we're going to be here a while I can turn it up."

"I don't know how long we'll be here. I don't know what I'm looking for."

"Okay, let's just leave our coats on then."

"How long had you been seeing Sammy?" I asked, then wondered if that was the right question. I mean, they'd been together long enough for Sammy to leave Phil a ginormous house.

"A little more than a year. We were friends forever and then... I'm sure you know how this happens. One day we looked at each other and bam! Everything changed."

I had absolutely no idea what that was like and I wasn't sure I wanted to. Vinnie was my friend precisely because I would *never* look at him and feel any sort of bam. Which reminded me, I really needed to call him. Phil was still talking—"I wanted to tell people. In fact, we'd been arguing about it a bit."

"Does the sheriff know you were involved with Sammy?" I asked. Somewhere, probably *CSI* or *Law & Order* or possibly *Police Academy*, I'd learned that the person most likely to kill you is a loved one. Phil hadn't confessed, but he was still a suspect.

"Well, no. Sammy wouldn't have liked that, and I want to honor his wishes. It's the least I can do." He glowered at me. "I don't think he was wrong, exactly. You may not understand this yet, but in a small town you don't advertise your relationships. It's just not wise."

Part of me wanted to say something, like how things would never get better if people weren't honest about who they were, but then I remembered I wasn't out to Nana Cole. I mean, sometimes I thought she had to know, right? I mean she couldn't be that clueless—

"Where do you want to start?"

"Oh. Well. It wasn't, like, a home invasion. I mean, the doors weren't broken down and the car wasn't stolen. So Sammy probably knew the person who killed him, right?"

"Yes. That's probably true. I don't like thinking about it though."

"Why not?"

"If Sammy knew his killer then I probably knew him too. I mean, *know* him. I don't want to think that someone I know killed Sammy."

"He may not have known them well," I said, trying to make Phil feel better. "You don't have to know someone well to let them into your house."

"That's true," Phil said. "Actually, it could have been someone posing as a door-to-door salesman. Sammy would have let them in, just to get them out of the cold."

Was there still such a thing as a door-to-door salesman? I'd never seen one. No, I didn't believe any of what we were saying. Sammy knew his killer and knew them well.

"Would they have stood here in the foyer?" I asked.

"No, they would have gone into the parlor."

"That's what he called it? The parlor."

"Well, it's a big house. There's the parlor and the living room. Sammy would have brought a guest into the parlor," he explained. He gestured toward the double doors on my left. He slid the pocket doors open. The room smelled like drying wood, furniture polish and dust, even though I couldn't see any dust. Everything was shiny and clean.

It looked as though Phil, or someone, had already been there to clean. If the police had kept the place shut up for six weeks, there would be dust. And if they'd searched, either before or after the body was found, there would be evidence of that.

The room in front of me could have been a showroom. There were two attractive but uncomfortable looking sofas in front of me. They were covered in the same geometric pattern, green and blue squares. Against one wall was a delicate desk, a tall side table against another, in front of us an elaborate tiled fireplace. I glanced at the brass and wrought iron fire set standing next to it, shiny and clean. Phil did good work—or whoever had cleaned the place.

On the coffee table between the sofas sat a bowl of marble balls, big six-inch balls. Were they all there? Or was one missing? On the mantle of the fireplace was a granite obelisk. Had there once been two?

Whatever Sammy had been hit with had probably been in the room. I mean, the killer wouldn't have shown up carrying a blunt instrument, right? They would have killed him with something at hand, something in the room. And they couldn't have simply put whatever it was back—it would have had blood on it and fingerprints. Even if the item had been cleaned, the blood could be detected—it only takes one episode of *CSI* to figure that out. Although, I doubted the Wyandot County sheriff was big on forensics.

"When you cleaned the room was it covered in fingerprint dust and other… um, stuff."

"How did you know—yes, it was." *Did this guy never watch TV?*

"Is anything missing? This is how many marble balls there always were? There was only one of these?" I asked, pointing at the obelisk.

"Everything seems to be here."

"Can I see the rest of the house?" I asked.

"But, you think he was killed in here?"

"I'm not sure. There would probably have been a lot of blood."

I hit my head on the toilet once and bled all over the place. I barely got it cleaned up before Vinnie came home, so I could imagine how much blood there would be if someone actually died.

"I didn't see any sign of blood," Phil said. "Anywhere."

So, who cleaned up Sammy's blood? I was back to the idea the killer might have an accomplice. Someone to help clean up and carry Sammy's body to the car.

"I don't mean to harp on this, but why didn't you come into the house when Sammy went missing? I mean, he didn't show up at his meeting, he couldn't be reached on the phone, wouldn't it make sense to check the house before you called the police? I mean, the sheriff."

"I was out of town. A book fair in Chicago. I left the day before he disappeared and then came back as soon as I heard."

"No one else had a key?"

"Not to my knowledge. Opal and Richard told me they knocked on the door, peeked in the windows, then they called the sheriff."

"How did they get in?"

"They didn't get in. I just said—"

"The sheriff, how did the sheriff get in?"

"Oh, well, I'm not entirely sure. Detective Lehmann just took over; he told Opal and Richard to go away."

"Detective Lehmann showed up? To check on someone? Why not a deputy?"

"When you put it that way, it does seem weird. But—well, I don't think there's a lot for him to do. This kind of thing doesn't happen often."

I'm not sure I believed that. It was more like this was a murder investigation right from the start even though it wasn't. Sammy had been thought missing. Missing people turned up all the time, so why would a detective—? Maybe they did things differently in the country. I had to keep that in mind.

I asked again to see the house and this time Phil showed me around. What he called the living room on the other side of the house was an even larger room, but it was more comfortable. It had a giant television and a sectional couch. It opened onto the dining room. Beyond that was a kitchen that had been wonderfully rehabbed.

"How long did Sammy own the house?"

"I think he bought it after his mother died. That would have been around eighty-eight, eighty-nine."

"So this isn't the house where he had the disco in the cellar?"

"No, that was just a ranch house out near Coldwater."

"Where is Coldwater again?"

"It's on Big Turtle Highway near Goose Lake."

That actually didn't help me. I'd have to look at the map when I got back to the truck.

"He lost that house after he was sent to prison," Phil continued.

"He was sent to prison? Why?" I wasn't sure it was at all relevant to finding his killer, but it was great gossip.

"The disco in his basement."

"That's illegal?"

"Gay sex was illegal then. Still is technically, so the sheriff then called it a bawdy house."

"Seriously? A bawdy house?" To me a bawdy house was, like, Shakespearean. "Isn't that the same as a whorehouse?"

"Prostitution or lewdness. That's how the statute is written. It was a huge scandal."

"But it was the seventies. I thought everything got better after Stonewall."

"Um, no. I mean things were starting to get better back then, well, in the cities, but the sheriff—"

"Sheriff Crocker?"

"No, this would be four or five sheriffs ago. Dill Crocker would have just been a deputy then."

"But do you think he was involved?"

He shrugged. "Probably.

I didn't know what to make of that. It seemed like something, but what? I mean, did the sheriff have a motive for killing Sammy? A very, very old motive?

A few minutes later, I gave up and we went back out to the Subaru. "Did Sammy leave you the car too?"

"He did. The house and all his personal property."

"So, why aren't you driving it?"

"Oh, um, probate—" he stopped and gathered himself. "That's not true. I'm just not ready. These few weeks... None of this seems real. I know people always say that but... I can't help but think he's coming back."

Chapter 9

THE THING I liked so much about Oxy was that all my problems—the student loan I wasn't paying, the hospital bill threatening to arrive, the maxed-out credit cards, the fact that I didn't really have a job and had no idea how I was ever going to go home—all the problems that were like giant, terrifying monsters when I was sober turned into docile, well-behaved little children when I was high. It was easy to tell them, 'Hey kids, go in the other room and play. Daddy's gonna mellow.'

After the trip to Sammy's house, I went back to Nana Cole's and tried to collect my thoughts about the murder. Or at least that was the plan. When I emptied my pockets into the gigantic ceramic ashtray that took up a corner of my mom's desk, I found a wadded-up tissue in with the keys and quarters. Inside the tissue were four and a half 10s. I must have gotten them from Bill Touhy, Manager. I'd only taken a half of one the night before—smart since I'd had a lot to drink.

Of course, he said I'd taken too many pills so there might have been six originally. I might have taken one and a half. That wouldn't have been as smart, well, not smart at all but it would explain my condition that morning. Seven would be even more explanatory.

I took an Oxy—plus the half for good measure—and went back downstairs. Nana Cole, who was out back doing something in her garden, had made banana bread. I cut off two slices, poured myself a glass of milk and went back upstairs.

Setting my snack on the desk, I let it sit there. Oxy was always better on an empty stomach. I'd have my snack after it took hold—if I remembered.

I couldn't believe that Sammy Hart had gotten put in jail for running a gay disco. In the seventies! I knew my history—well, maybe I didn't, but I had seen the movie *54* and just completely loved it. I mean Studio 54 wasn't *exactly* a gay disco, but it wasn't exactly not. And it did count as history. Kind of.

So how that kind of place could be completely okay in one part of the country and the kind of place that got you thrown in jail in another part, well, it just didn't make any sense.

But I was losing focus. I had to find Sammy's killer and the fact that he'd spent time in prison for running a bawdy house something like thirty years ago didn't really have anything to do with it. Did it?

Had I learned anything at all by visiting Sammy's house? I guess I learned that he had a lot of money, but I'd sort of learned that at Mr. Chips. I did learn that he was romantically involved with Phil and that it was some kind of secret. I didn't want to think about that too much. Two middle-aged guys. Old people sex. Nobody would kill over old people sex. That just made no sense.

The Oxy had begun to kick in. I knew the high would have come even faster if I'd crushed the pill and snorted it, but that was something addicts did and I was not going to cross that line. I could be patient. I was a casual user. In fact, I barely took drugs at all compared to some people I knew in L.A. I knew people who took a lot—

I realized I wasn't going to be able to focus on the Sammy Hart thing, so I got in front of my iBook and turned on Netscape to do a little web surfing, which mostly meant reading the personals on *Craigslist*. They were sad. Really sad.

Somewhere along the line, I took another Oxy and curled up on my bed with Reilly to watch my DVD of *Bridget Jones' Diary*. Truth be told, I loved fat Renee so much more than skinny Renee. Soon, I lost track of where the movie was going even though I'd seen it like a hundred—

I woke up the next morning around eleven-thirty. I was still dressed. My iBook was dead since the plug had detached and it had been running on battery power for who knows how long. The banana bread sat on my desk looking kind of stale. I checked my little stash and saw that I had one lonely Oxy left. I must have taken more, even though I didn't remember doing it.

I had to take Reilly out. He hadn't been out in, well, I couldn't figure out how long. Numbly, I picked my way downstairs, Reilly on my heels. My boots and my jacket were by the kitchen door. When I got to the kitchen, I saw Nana Cole sitting there with three other ladies. I'd met them before, I think. One of them, at least. There was a rotating cast of women who came for coffee, muffins and a bit of knitting after church.

I smiled and waved as I went by. I was out the door in two seconds. The day was glorious, sky bright blue with a few puffy clouds. And warm. It was suddenly warm. Squinting at the sun, I could barely believe that just a few weeks before it had been deep winter. Reilly went off and did his business then came back to me. He stood staring at me.

"Are you ready to go inside?" I asked. I didn't actually get an answer, but when I moved to go back to the house he followed. I opened the kitchen door and we went in.

"Well, I don't know. I just don't think it's nice," Dorothy said. She was nearly sixty and in need of dental work. Next to her was a knitting bag, and she was in the midst of knitting something very yellow.

"It's what's in the bible," another woman said. I think her name was Jan. She was the youngest and very conservatively dressed. "I think that settles it."

"Yes, but it also says we should stone an adulteress to death," Dorothy said, knitting needles clicking. "We're not going to do that, are we?"

"I wouldn't mind," Nana Cole said.

"Besides," Jan said. "Even though we don't stone adulterers

anymore that doesn't mean they're okay. They're still wrong in the eyes of the Lord."

"Yes, but we don't *do* anything about it."

"Dorothy, we're supposed to turn the other cheek."

"Well, I don't think that means every single time."

I went to the pantry and got out a can of Reilly's food. I scooped all of it into a bowl for him and mixed in some dry.

"You missed an interesting sermon, Henry," said Jan. She said that every Sunday she came. I doubted it was ever true.

"That's okay," I said, since I didn't want to hear them talking about it.

"Come and sit down with us," Jan said. "Have a cup of tea."

"I really have things I need to—"

"Whatever it is, it can wait," Nana Cole said.

Uncomfortably, I was too fuzzy to fight back so I sat down. Nana Cole got up and found me a teacup in the cupboard. It was yellow and said UCLA in blue. My alma mater. I'd sent it to her freshman year. Now, she'd decided it was *my* cup.

"The reverend was talking about Sammy Hart," Jan said. "The man whose body you found. He said that Sammy deserved what he got."

"He didn't exactly say that," Nana Cole corrected.

"He came damn close."

"Kind of goes against the whole idea of loving your neighbor," I pointed out.

Nana Cole glared at me while she poured hot water in my cup.

"I really don't think that means *all* neighbors. That would be excessive," Dorothy said. "Not everything in the Bible should be taken literally."

"Just the things you believe," I said almost under my breath.

"Barbara, what do you hear from your grandson?" Nana Cole asked in a diplomatic change of subject. "It's Josh, isn't it?"

Barbara was near Nana Cole's age, her hair white and thinning. She hadn't said anything yet, and maybe this was why.

"Yes, Josh is in Baghdad. Things are going well, I think." She paused and bit her lip as she did. "I—I'm getting worried that they haven't found those weapons yet, the ones they said were there."

"Oh, that doesn't make any difference," Nana Cole said.

"But that's the whole reason we're at war. If they lied to us—well, my grandson's life is in danger right now. What is all this for if not to protect us? What if I lose my grandson over a lie?"

"Barbara, that's not what's happening," Nana Cole said. "Mr. Bush knows what he's doing. Just because the Democrats have made it seem like he doesn't can't make it true. They want you to doubt him. So don't. The president knows lots of things we can't know. Secrets. Everything he's doing he has a good reason for even if we can't see it. Maybe they've even found the weapons and they just can't tell us, have you thought of that? Going there was the right thing. Don't worry."

This was very different from the things my friends in L.A. said. They called it a war for oil. One guy I sort of knew sold his SUV because it got bad gas mileage and he didn't feel right being against the war and driving it. That was extreme.

"I'm not sure I believe that anymore, Emma," Barbara said in a very quiet voice. "I'm not sure the war is right."

The women all looked at each other uncomfortably. I sugared my tea.

"Well, maybe it's time to go," Jan said.

"You're my ride so I guess that means me too," Dorothy said.

"I should be the one to go," Barbara said. After all, she'd had the nerve to disagree with Nana Cole.

"No one needs to run off," Nana Cole said.

"It *is* getting late, though," Jan said. "My boys will be expecting Sunday supper. I need to get to work."

Nana Cole and I stood up while the women left. She walked to the door and watched them as they went out to their cars. After we were alone, we sat back down. I had a full mug of tea, so it was a hard to sneak up to my room. I mean, I could have taken the cup upstairs, but it would be obvious I didn't want to—

"Nana, you said Sammy Hart was a Beckett. Can you tell me more about the Becketts?"

"Sure. They're one of the founding families. My grandmother was a Beckett."

"She was? Then why don't you own half the county?"

"She would have been born in the 1870s or the 1880s. I'm not sure she *could* have inherited. And even if she could, it wouldn't have been uncommon for the family to leave her nothing."

"That's harsh," I said.

She shrugged. "Women got dowrys then. You got your share at the beginning of your marriage."

"Except you didn't get it. Your husband did."

She smiled as though she knew something I didn't. "People today think marriage is a partnership, but that's two people. Marriage makes one person. One flesh."

That made me glad it would never be legal for me to get married. I didn't want to be one person with someone else. Anyone else.

"I guess that's why women jump on their husband's funeral pyre in India," I said.

She looked up and scowled at me. The primary use of my college education so far was antagonizing my grandmother.

"Well, that's just barbaric."

"But if you lost half of yourself how do you survive?"

She pursed her lips. "You're thinking about this all wrong. It's not like your grandfather and I were Siamese twins and he was surgically—"

Her eyes filled with tears and she stopped.

"What?"

"I'm wrong. That's exactly what it felt like when I lost him. Like he'd been ripped away."

This was uncomfortable. Of all the times I would have loved hearing her say she was wrong this wasn't one of them. I'd made an old lady cry, I needed to get back on course.

"So, if we're Becketts that means that we're related to

Sammy Hart?" I resisted the temptation to ask why she hadn't told me I'd stumbled over the body of a relative.

"I wouldn't say we're Becketts, the connection goes back quite a way. Sammy was my third or fourth cousin. Something like that. We're related to the Shecks too, by the way."

"Wait. I found a dead relative on a relative's property?"

"My maiden name is Scheck, except with a C. It's a German name. That side of the family, the Apple Lane Shecks, they dropped the C during World War One. They didn't want to seem so German. My side kept it. It caused a big riff."

"And you're still holding a grudge."

"No, of course not."

"Is there anyone in the Beckett family who might want to see Sammy dead?"

She thought for a moment. "Well, yes, I suppose. It's a large family. And Sammy was, well, different."

"And Sammy had money."

"That came from the Hart side."

"Really, I just assumed—"

"Oh yeah, I think everyone does. There was a lot of pressure on Colleen not to leave it all to Sammy after the trouble he had. But he was the last of the Harts and her son, of course."

"He was her only child?"

"Yes."

We were quiet. I wondered what she knew about the 'the trouble he had.' I wasn't sure I wanted to ask. It hit a little close to home. I know it was silly not to come out to her, but my mother had specifically told me not to—yet another reason we weren't on speaking terms. She'd told me I had to go back in the closet.

"What kind of trouble did Sammy get into?" I asked. I had to. I was too curious.

She blushed but then said, "They say he was running some kind of sex ring in Coldwater. And it must be true. He went to prison for it."

"He was running a disco out of his basement."

"A disco? How would you know that?"

"Opal told me. She was a friend of his."

"She's too young to know. No one goes to prison for running a disco. That's absurd."

I didn't say anything. I didn't think there was a way to make her believe something she'd already decided wasn't true.

"Why are you so interested anyway?"

"I found his body," I said. "And now you tell me he's a relative."

And the reward. But that was the last thing in the world I wanted to tell her about. I didn't want her to know I needed it to get the heck out of there. There would be plenty of time to tell her once I got my hands on it.

"You never ask about your mother."

"I'm sure she's fine. Her new boy—"

"Not now. When she was young. When she lived here. You don't ask about that."

I didn't ask because I really didn't want to talk about my mother at all. Ever. But obviously, Nana Cole had something she wanted to say about her. I took the bait.

"What was she like, then?"

"If you think you're trouble, you're nothing compared to your mother. Boys, booze, drugs. You name it and she was doing it by the time she was sixteen. They say the apple doesn't fall far from the tree but not in this case. In our case the apple fell in another county entirely."

I could have disagreed with that. Rigid, immovable, opinionated, manipulative, stubborn, difficult: these were all things Nana Cole had in common with my mother. The apple fell a lot closer to the tree than the tree would like to acknowledge.

Chapter 10

MONDAY MORNING BEV called far earlier than I would have liked and asked me to come in to help put together the annual report. I tried to demure, "Oh, I don't know anything about annual reports."

Well, I didn't. Not really.

"Your grandmother told me you have a degree in communications, you need to help me communicate."

I knew that degree was going to bite me in the ass. I'd only gotten it because most of the classes I needed were super easy. Not to mention, I was in L.A. and it sounded vaguely film-y. Of course, it wasn't. Not really.

Behind The Conservancy offices was a parking lot with room for four or five cars. When I got there, only one space was available, so I took it. I could have gone around to the front of the building and parked on Main, but there was something official about parking in the back. And the walk was shorter.

One of the white Ford Explorers the sheriff's department used was parked across the far end of the tiny lot blocking the cars in. Bev's bronze Jeep Cherokee from the '80s sat with its doors open and its back hatch flipped up. A string bean of a deputy was picking through the car. Okay, that was weird.

I walked into the office and saw there were stacks of papers everywhere. Bev was on the computer working on a compli-cated looking spreadsheet.

"What's going on?"

"Oh, nothing. The sheriff got a tip. They come through every few months. Someone tells them I'm selling pot out of the back of my Jeep—they think that's why we conserve land. To grow pot. Ridiculous, of course. The climate's all wrong. Anyway, the sheriff has to check it out."

"That's crazy."

"Not everyone likes what we're doing. They think it lowers the tax base. Ironically, it's the people who don't want to pay taxes at all who are maddest about that."

"Is that how everything is done around here? Anonymous tips?"

"What do you mean?"

"We got that note about the cars."

"Oh yeah. I didn't even think about that. Um, I don't think there's a connection. I've been anonymously accused of growing marijuana before. I mean, I *should* be growing marijuana. I've heard it's good for epilepsy."

"Oh, you have epilepsy?" That explained the Dilantin and Valium in her purse. I reminded myself to check later to see if she'd refilled her Valium prescription. If she had, I could nab a couple of pills. Not as fun as Oxy, but it would do in a pinch.

"Yeah, I was in a car accident about fifteen years ago. But I haven't had a fit in almost a year, so it's going well."

Uh, yeah. Given the amount of Valium she was taking that was no surprise.

"Okay, good," I said. "So, I heard that Sammy Hart is leaving some land to The Conservancy?"

"How do you know that?"

"I talked to Phil, the guy who's his executor."

She shrugged, deciding she might as well talk about it. "It's a hundred and twenty acres that fronts on Goose Lake. It's going to protect about a quarter of the lake. It's a wonderful parcel. We're lucky to get it."

"That's worth a lot of money," I said, thinking of all the vacation homes that could be built on it.

"It's an important eco-system. You can't put a price on that. Besides, the other lots around Goose Lake will actually be more valuable because we're protecting so much."

I doubted a developer would see it quite like that. Or a real estate agent.

The deputy pushed the door open. He wasn't much older than I was. His face had a lot of freckles and I suspected under his hat his hair was orange. Even though it was hovering around freezing, he'd taken his jacket off and a tag on his chest said, DANLY.

"All set?" Bev asked.

"Um, can you explain this?" Deputy Danly asked, holding up a wrought iron fireplace poker in a latex-gloved hand.

"I've never seen that before in my life," Bev said. "I don't have a fireplace. Or even a wood stove."

"There's blood and hair on the point."

"Oh my God! And you found that in my Jeep?"

"Under the front seat."

"Well—*I* didn't put it there."

"Bev, you should probably come with me down to the sheriff's office," he said.

"Am I under arrest?"

"I don't know that we want to go that far unless we have to."

She looked at me and asked, "Can you stay here? Just until I get back or until four if I don't…"

"Sure," I said. "Um, Deputy, who do you think was hit with the poker?"

"I don't know. But Sammy Hart was hit with something."

"I was at Sammy's house on Saturday, though, and the whole fireplace set was there. In fact, it doesn't even look like that one. The one I saw at the house was brass and wrought iron."

He looked a little confused. I think the conversation was above his pay grade.

"Well somebody was struck with this one. Pretty hard. We're going to need to figure this out."

Bev put on her coat and picked up her purse. "All right. I'm ready to go. Although, honestly, I don't know what I can tell you."

"You need to speak to Detective Lehmann."

"Right," she said. Then she leaned over to me and said, "Don't tell a soul about this. I'm sure it'll all be worked out in a couple of hours."

"Right."

"I mean it, no one."

"Okay."

The moment she was out the door, I called Nana Cole.

"Bev has been arrested for murder," I said breathlessly.

"What?!"

"The deputy was just here, he searched her car and found a bloody fireplace poker. He thinks she killed Sammy Hart."

"Oh my God! That's ridiculous. Bev would never!"

"Do you think she needs a lawyer?"

"Don Livingstone does all the work for The Conservancy pro bono. I'll call him."

"Okay, but she told me not to tell anyone."

"Well that's just foolish. Thank you for calling me, dear."

She hung up. I wondered who else I should call. Yeah, yeah, yeah, she'd just told me not to tell anyone. But she couldn't have meant Nana Cole and she certainly didn't mean—

"Vinnie?" I said when the line was picked up.

"Ubba, gubba," he said.

"Vinnie, wake up. My boss just got arrested for murder."

That woke him. "Where the hell are you? Wasn't the whole idea to get you out of the big bad city so you'd be safe?"

"Yeah, I don't think that's working out. Also, I may have sort of, kind of, had sex for drugs."

"Moochie! You need to come back to L.A. Small town life is corrupting you."

"I didn't tell you, there's a reward for whoever solves the murder."

"Which murder? People seem to be getting killed there left and right."

"There's only one murder. So far. Anyway, there's a reward and I've decided to get it—oh, and another thing I didn't tell you. The body I found. He's like my cousin. And, the place where I found him—the people who own it, they're my cousins too."

"Are you in Appalachia?"

"I mean, they're really distant cousins. We don't even call them family."

"My God, Moochie. Don't sleep with anyone else. It could be incest and you'd have no idea."

"I know, right? I need to stay focused and find the killer, so I can get the reward and come home."

"Uh-huh."

He sounded dubious. I couldn't blame him. I mean, I sometimes had trouble remembering what was in a macchiato. Still, I was about to protest and explain that I was actually doing very well at finding things out—or at least I thought I was—when there was a beep on the line.

"I have another call. Let me see who—"

"Darling, take your call. Let me go back to sleep." Before I could answer he'd hung up. I clicked over to the other call.

"Hello?"

"Henry, this is Opal."

That was odd. Why was *she*—

"How did you get this phone number?"

"You gave it to me before you left Mr. Chips. I mean you were totally sloshed. You left with Billy Touhy. God knows why."

I was completely humiliated for a moment. To save face, I changed the subject. "Something's happening. They just arrested Bev."

"Bev Jenkins? From The Conservancy?"

"Yes. That Bev." How many Bevs were there in Wyandot County? "They think she killed Sammy."

"That's—Why would she kill Sammy?"

"I don't know. They were searching her car because someone called in a tip about her selling marijuana—"

"Oh, that's stupid. Everyone knows Ronnie Sheck sells most of the weed around here. And no one ever searches his car."

I was tempted to ask for his number but continued on anyway. "They found an iron poker in her car, you know, for a fireplace. The deputy said it had blood and hair on the end. That's how Sammy was killed."

"So that's why they think Bev killed him?"

"I don't know if they think anything yet. The thing is I was at the house Saturday and there was a poker—" Then I had an idea. An important idea. "I wonder if someone replaced the set?"

"What?"

"If this is the poker that killed Sammy, it should be missing from his living room. But it's not. There's a nice set there. In fact, it looks brand new. Do you think Phil would have noticed the poker was missing and just replaced the set?"

"No. That doesn't make sense."

She was sort of right. I mean, let's say the killer held onto the poker so they could implicate Bev. They wouldn't have wanted to replace the set at Sammy's house, that would just confuse things. And Phil, he wouldn't have replaced the set since the fact that the poker was missing was important. So, who had replaced it? And why? Was it the same person who cleaned up the blood that should have been at the scene?

"So, why were you calling me?"

"Well, I thought you should know. I told you that Sammy was seeing someone and I didn't know who. Well, it was Richard."

"Richard?" That was a surprise, I was sure she was going to say Phil.

"Obviously, the fact that Sammy was seeing someone had nothing to do with the murder. I mean, Richard is the last person in the world—"

"He was upset that Sammy left his house to Phil, wasn't he?"

"What? No. Richard hates that house. And he has his own. Or at least he did. I think it might be in—"

"Still, Richard isn't mentioned in the will *at all*. And Phil is."

I didn't really want to tell her that Phil was also involved with Sammy. I didn't trust Opal not to claim the reward for herself, and if it turned out that one of them—

"That would be really petty, and even if Richard is a little upset that doesn't mean he killed Sammy."

"No, but it does mean he had a motive."

"But we tried for weeks and weeks to find Sammy. Richard was upset the whole time. He wasn't faking that."

That made me think of something. "When did Sammy disappear?"

"In February."

"What day?"

"The nineteenth.

Bev had a calendar pinned to the wall. It was given out by Wyandot Landscaping and Nursery. Keeping the phone cradled between my shoulder and neck, I took the calendar off the wall and flipped back to February. On the nineteenth, Bev had made a note that said, GRAND RAPIDS.

"I knew it."

"Knew what?" Opal wanted to know.

"February nineteenth is the day I got here. Bev drove down to Grand Rapids with my grandmother. They probably left here right after lunch and we didn't get back until well after dinner. I think Sammy was killed during that time. If I'm right, then she couldn't have done it."

"Well, you didn't really think she did, did you?"

"No. But someone's trying to make it look like she did."

"Why? Why would someone do that?"

"I don't know."

Chapter 11

TWENTY MINUTES LATER, a tow truck showed up. The heavy-set, middle-aged driver got out and started to hitch up Bev's Jeep. I went out and asked, "What are you doing? That's a legal parking space."

"I've got orders to take this vehicle over to the state police lab in Grayling."

"Grayling? Where's that?"

He pointed kind of east and said, "About eighty miles that way."

"Do you have a warrant?"

"I don't. But somebody does. They don't call me until they've got one."

I kind of wanted to insist on seeing the warrant, but I figured this guy was right. They probably did have a warrant. And if they didn't they could get one soon enough. I mean, a murder weapon had been found in the Jeep. That had to be enough probable cause to get a warrant so they could go over the rest of the car with a fine-tooth comb. And besides, Bev had said they could look in the car in the first place.

I turned around and went back inside. Bev was going to be fine. My nana was sending a lawyer and she had an alibi even if she didn't know it yet. I sat down and asked myself the really important question: Was any of this helping me find the killer? I desperately needed the reward and didn't want to get distracted. Distracted meant I'd be staying and that was not okay.

Someone was trying to frame Bev. Why? If it was the killer —and it probably was—it was so he wouldn't get caught. Well, of course, he didn't want to get caught. And one of the best ways not to get caught is for someone else to get caught. But why Bev? Or was that even important?

I had no idea. Absolutely no idea.

The phone began to ring. The first call went terribly wrong. It was one of the donors who'd heard Bev had gotten arrested and she wanted to know if it was for embezzlement and could she get her money returned. I had no clue what to say to that, other than "No comment."

When I hung the phone up, it rang again almost immediately. I didn't answer. Instead, I wrote out a simple statement that said, "Bev Jenkins has not been arrested. She is currently at the sheriff's office assisting with an investigation. We expect that she'll be back at her desk tomorrow morning. If you need to speak with her directly please call back."

Now I was ready to answer the phone. It was a grueling couple of hours, but I stuck to my script. People tried to interrupt me, I didn't let them. They asked additional questions, I didn't answer them. If they really annoyed me I read the statement twice. Eventually, the calls slowed down. Word probably got around that I wasn't going to say much of anything. People must have just given up.

By one o'clock I was starving. I locked up the office and went around the building out to Main Street. The commercial area of Masons Bay Village was almost exclusively on Main Street and extended for about three blocks. It was similar to Bellflower but about a quarter of the size. There were five restaurants in that tiny area: Elaine's Table, which was high end; Main Street Café, which was cheaper but didn't have any takeout; Siam Palace, which served the worst Thai food I'd ever had; Beanie's Bakery, that served a really yummy breakfast biscuit but had nothing for lunch except muffins; and a pizza place called Little Italy.

There were no McDonald's, Burger Kings or Kentucky Fried Chickens. The village had banned them. In fact, they were noticeably absent from most of the county. I almost gave up, but then I remembered that Cuppa Mud—an unfortunately named coffee shop—had sandwiches and croissants. I went there and got in line. The people in front of me were discussing Bev's arrest.

"I'm not surprised. Liberals have no morals."

"Evie, how do you even know she's a liberal?"

"Come on, she's a conservationist. They put nature before people."

Her friend was trying to be polite. "People are part of nature."

"Oh, that's the silliest thing I've ever heard."

When it was my turn, I ordered a tuna sandwich, a pain au chocolat and a sixteen-ounce mocha latte. I was going to put in a lot of hours this week so I could afford to splurge. Okay, well, actually I couldn't or shouldn't, one or the other, but I was going to anyway.

Cuppa Mud was clean (ironically) and recently remodeled using a lot of raw wood. I sat and ate my lunch in front of one of its big windows. There were people around, of course. The ones who sort of knew who I was peeked at me with curiosity. The ones who had no idea acted like I didn't even exist. I really preferred the second group. When I got back to The Conservancy, Sandy Edelson was waiting at the door.

"I heard that Bev's been arrested, what I can do to help?"

"She hasn't been arrested. She's at the sheriff's office assisting —" I realized I was following my phone script. "It's going to be fine. She'll be back soon."

"What happened?"

Letting us into the office, I brought Sandy up to speed on the morning. I probably wasn't supposed to, but I figured if I didn't tell her she'd just end up with all the wrong information. If people are going to gossip they should gossip about true things.

"I know who the woman is who was fighting with Sammy."

"You do? Who was she?"

"Her name is Audrey."

I waited but then it seemed like only the name Audrey was coming. "Audrey what?"

"Audrey who works at The Co-op."

"Okay," I said. That did make her a little easier to find.

"I was doing my shopping and there she was behind the checkout."

"Did you say anything to her?"

"God no. She might be a killer."

That was a good point, but I didn't think even a murderer was likely to attack someone in the middle of a food co-operative. Even a vicious one.

"Did you at least get a good look at her?"

"Her normal aura is red. People with red auras can be quick to anger. If she killed Sammy she did it in a moment of passion. But she's not naturally an evil person."

"Uh-huh. Is she tall or short? Skinny or fat?"

"Medium height, a little heavy. Sorry. I forget that not everyone sees auras."

"That's all right."

She studied the air around me. "You have a yellow aura, dark yellow but lighter in places."

Great. My aura was the color of piss.

"Do you want to know what that means?" Before I could say no she went on, "You've lost something, maybe a lot. You're desperate to achieve a goal. You're a student of life. When you accept that, your aura will improve."

"Well that would be good. I don't think yellow really goes with my skin tone."

"You don't believe me. That's okay, I'm used to it," she said, remarkably calm. "I'm sorry. I'm taking up your time."

"No, this is very helpful. I mean, the part about Audrey. I'm glad you told me."

"Should I go to the sheriff?"

"Oh, you know, I think maybe I should talk to Audrey. It

could be something completely unrelated. We don't want to get the poor woman in trouble for no reason."

I felt like an asshole. I really just wanted to hog the reward. I mean, Sandy lived in a trailer so she probably needed the money as much as I did. But that didn't mean I wanted to give it to her.

"Well, I should go," Sandy said. "If Audrey *is* the killer, would you let me know?"

"Of course," I said. Meaning as soon as I got the reward in my pocket. Maybe right before it comes out in the *Wyandot Eagle*.

After Sandy left, I called the sheriff's office and asked for Detective Lehmann. If this did lead to Sammy's killer I wanted to be on record as the one who'd discovered it. When Lehmann came to the phone I said, "Sammy Hart was seen arguing with a woman a couple of days before he disappeared."

"Yeah, so what?"

"The woman is named Audrey and she works at The Co-op."

I could almost hear him getting angry. "And you want me to drop everything and go accuse her of murder?"

Well, to be honest, it *had* crossed my mind.

"You should at least talk to her, shouldn't you?"

He hung up on me, which I thought was very rude. That left me sitting there with nothing to do. A half hour passed, and out of boredom I began looking at the stacks of paper. They didn't make a lot of sense.

What did make sense was the 2001 annual report. I gathered Bev was working on fiscal year 2002 which must have closed on March 31st. The report—which was really a fancy brochure with lots of pretty photos—was actually light on numbers. The piles of paper and the spreadsheet Bev was working on were obviously the backup behind the copy, what little there was. It seemed like she was working on not only how much they'd taken in and spent, but how much acreage they had under easement and how much they owned outright, how many volunteers they had, and how many members there were on the roster. Stuff people would want to know, I guess.

In my original conversation with Bev she'd told me everything The Conservancy did, but honestly, I hadn't paid much attention. I think I was in shock. I'd only been here a few days and just the week before my life in L.A. had been moving steadily along. Words like stewardship, easement, watershed and wetlands didn't mean a whole lot to me. Now, reading the brochure, I saw that The Conservancy led nature walks, protected farmland so that it stayed farmland and didn't become tract housing, planted native plants—I was kind of clueless about that, I thought plants just grew where they were supposed to. Anyway, the long and the short of it was that The Conservancy did a lot. Tons.

I decided not to get involved with the numbers, that was all kind of fuzzy. But as director of The Wyandot County Land Conservancy, Bev had written an introduction to the annual report and it was just, well, not good. Flat, boring, dull. I decided the most help I could be would be to draft out a better intro for 2002. One with a little more pizzazz.

After working on it for an hour, I thought I had a pretty good couple of crackling paragraphs. Better than 2001, that was for sure. Of course, she'd need to reference some of the numbers she was putting together, but she could slot those in later.

Around three, one of the sheriff's Explorers drove up and dropped Bev off. She'd barely shut the passenger door when it sped off. I hurried out.

"Are you okay?"

"Oh, I'm just fine."

"They towed your Jeep away."

"Yes, I know. They said they were going to."

"Was it awful?" I asked.

She didn't answer me. Instead, she said, "I think we should close up for the day."

"All right. I guess you need a ride home?"

"Your grandmother wants me to come to dinner."

"She does?"

"Don Livingstone was under strict instructions to get me released by dinnertime."

"I guess he's a good lawyer."

"I wasn't actually charged. Nobody around here locks their cars, so it would have been easy for any one of two thousand people to slip that poker underneath my seat. You should have seen people freak out when the deputy repeated what you'd said about there being a new fireplace set in the house." She rolled her eyes, continuing, "Sheriff Crocker nearly had a stroke. Especially when your name kept coming up."

"My name?"

"You've been spending time with Sammy's friends. They find that suspicious."

They'd probably be even more suspicious if they knew I was asking a lot of questions, particularly of Sammy's friends.

"I have to make friends with somebody, right?"

Bev gave me a funny look and I wondered how much she knew about Sammy's friends and Mr. Chips.

I glanced away and asked, "Are you ready?" That was the thing about being in the closet, you could always avert a crisis by changing the subject.

"Don't make the wrong friends, Henry. It's the same as making enemies."

Chapter 12

NANA COLE'S farm was a ten-minute ride from downtown Masons Bay, so we arrived quickly. Bev didn't say a whole lot on the way, other than that she needed a drink. I didn't blame her. I could have used a drink too. And a nice fat Oxy. Or several.

The wind was blowing strong and cold. I called for Reilly a couple of times and he came running. Instead of jumping on me though, he jumped on Bev. I told him to get down a couple of times and he ignored me.

"Off," Bev said, making a downward motion with her hand. He instantly obeyed. My dog was better trained than I thought. Or maybe I was the one who needed to be trained. Nah, I think he just liked Bev.

"I bought an Amish chicken. I just put it in," my grandmother said when we walked into the kitchen.

"You're kidding, I didn't know chickens had religious beliefs."

"Oh, stop it," Nana Cole said. "You know exactly what an Amish chicken is."

I did. There were some Amish nearby and they raised chickens. Their religious attachment to the nineteenth century meant the chickens were organic and treated humanely. Or at least that's what I assumed.

To Bev she said, "This one thinks he's funny." She gave Bev a tight hug. "I'm roasting the chicken with some of last year's garlic. Would you like a glass of white wine? Or do you want to start with something stronger?"

"Bourbon. If you have some."

She did. An entire shelf in the overstocked pantry was devoted to alcohol. More than a dozen partly drunk bottles of just about anything you could think of.

"I've got some Vernors if you want a highball," Nana Cole offered.

"That would be good. Thanks."

Nana Cole made the drink while I fed Reilly. He'd been nosing around Bev. Normally, she liked to scratch his head and he knew that. Today she didn't seem in the mood, so I thought I'd distract him.

"Reilly, come here," I said, putting down his dish. He rushed over to eat.

"So," Nana Cole said, sitting down. She'd already poured herself a glass of wine but didn't bother asking me if I'd like one. "What happened with the sheriff?"

I got myself a wine glass and poured myself some as I sat down to listen.

"Well, from the questions they were asking me, they got it in their heads I might have killed Sammy so that The Conservancy would inherit the land in his will."

"That's just ridiculous," Nana Cole said. "The Conservancy is not-for-profit. You wouldn't kill someone to *not* make money."

"Honestly, we're nearly to the point where we've got more than we can manage. I mean, we will. Manage it. I'll put on more staff. But we don't have a lot of cash on hand. I mean, people are more likely to give us land, so it can be difficult."

"You said Sammy's land is worth a lot," I said. "That sounds like a motive to kill him and a reason to frame you."

"I don't think so," Bev said. "Let's say they put me in prison for killing Sammy. The Conservancy would still get the land."

"Would they?" I wondered. I was pretty sure you weren't supposed to benefit by killing someone. So, if you were in someone's will and then you killed them—and got caught—you didn't get the money. I could see where this was a little different. The not-for-profit didn't kill him. But did the killer see it that way? A motive didn't have to be true to be a motive.

"Couldn't the will be contested?" I asked.

"It could be, I suppose."

We were quiet for a moment.

"Well, I'm going to write a letter to the *Wyandot Eagle*. Sheriff Crocker can't get away with this. They treated you like a criminal."

"Detective Lehmann tried to tell me my fingerprints were on that poker," Bev said. "Of course, they weren't. Before they let me go he admitted there weren't any fingerprints on there at all."

"What a thing to say to you," Nana Cole said. "It's just wrong."

"But there was hair and blood?" I asked. "On the poker?"

Bev nodded. "Yes, I think that part was true. It's going to take a while to know for sure, but they seem sure it will match Sammy."

"Well, there certainly haven't been any *other* murders in the county," Nana rightly pointed out.

"The tip about the marijuana in the Jeep came from the killer," I said. "And the tip about the cars did too."

"You mean, you think they wanted the body found just like they wanted the poker found," Bev said.

"Well, yes," I said. "If the killer thinks they're going to get that land at the end of this, they'd need Sammy's body to be found and they'd also need you to be arrested." Something dawned on me just then. "And then they'd need a lawyer to try and break the will."

"Lawyers are always at the bottom of everything." Nana Cole poured herself more wine. Her cheeks were already bright red.

"I wonder if they've already talked to a lawyer?" Bev frowned as she said it.

"They might have," I said. "I can ask Phil if he's been contacted by anyone."

"Phil who?" Nana Cole asked.

"I don't know his last name. He owns Village Books. He's Sammy executor."

"How do you know that?"

"He's a friend of Opal's."

"Are you seeing that girl?" she asked, her tone sounding unpleasant. She wouldn't like it if I was seeing Opal and she wouldn't like it if she knew the reason I wasn't seeing Opal.

"It's not serious," I said, deciding to let her chew on the situation for a while.

The air was uncomfortably thick for a moment. "I should walk Reilly," I said. He did like to go out after he ate a meal.

"Henry," Bev said. "You know, you might have over-complicated things. Whoever killed Sammy may just want to get away with it. If they knew The Conservancy was in the will, they might have wanted to pin it on me so it didn't get pinned on them. It could be that simple."

I thought about that for a moment. It actually made sense. Maybe she was right. Maybe I was over-complicating it.

"Okay, I guess I'll think about that."

"You don't need to think about it, Henry," Nana Cole said. "It's not your business."

Ignoring that, I led my dog out of the house.

———

DINNER WAS DELICIOUS. Nana Cole's chicken was wonderfully garlic-y, the mashed potatoes cheesy, the gravy rich and creamy. There was a salad too, but mostly I pushed that around my plate.

"We took the palace in Baghdad today," Nana Cole said.

"Emma, no war talk. Not today."

"Of course," she said. "I just, well, it's good news. That's why I brought it up."

We took a break before Nana Cole was going to bring out

peach pie and ice cream. Bev, who'd stuck with her highball throughout the meal, stood up, wobbling a bit. "Emma, I'm going to the little girl's room.

"You know where it is."

I'd had a lot of wine—though not as much as my nana—so as soon as Bev was down the hall, I asked, "You support The Conservancy but that seems to go against the rest of your beliefs."

She shook her head automatically, "No. No, it doesn't."

"Conservation is crunchy liberal."

"Oh, it is not. In my book, people can do what they want with their land and that includes giving it to The Conservancy."

"What about business though?"

"A farm is a business. When I die there will be an easement on this farm, you and your mother will only be able to sell it as a farm. It would break my heart to see a bunch of identical little cracker box houses spring up on this land. Some wannabe suburb stuck out in the middle of nowhere. No, I want the farm to keep going. If neither you or your mother want it, I still want it to continue."

"So you are leaving an easement to The Conservancy?"

"Don't tell Bev," she whispered. "I want her to be surprised."

The toilet flushed, and Bev came back down the hallway, managing to bounce off the wall only once. She stopped and giggled.

"Bev, are you all right?"

"Oh yes, I'm fine."

"I'm going to put you in the sewing room for the night," Nana Cole said.

"Oh you don't need to do that. I should go home. My cat—"

"That old cat couldn't care less if you're there or not."

"That's not true, Mr. Bumbles loves me."

"He loves that you feed him."

Bev looked for a moment like she might argue, but then she said, "Well, that might be true."

"Call your neighbor and have her go over and feed the cat."

She took her seat at the table again, took a big swig of her drink and said, "We haven't figured out who killed Sammy yet." That gave me the impression she'd just convinced herself she did have to stay.

"I'm sure the sheriff will figure it out soon enough," Nana Cole said.

"I don't think so," Bev said. "I don't think so at all."

"Do either of you know Audrey?" I asked.

"What? Audrey who?" Bev asked.

"Audrey who works at The Co-op."

Nana Cole and Bev looked at each other as they thought. "One of the cashiers?" Nana Cole asked.

"Yes. Do you know her last name?"

"No. No. She's not one of the old families."

"Oh, I know who you mean," Bev said. "I think she was raised here but Emma's right. She's not one of the old families. Why are we talking about her?"

"Sandy Edelson saw Audrey—"

"Sandy Edelson? Now who's that?" Nana Cole asked. I had the feeling she didn't have too many conversations about people she hadn't known since birth. "You seem to know a lot of women all of a sudden—"

"You wouldn't know her," Bev said. "She bought that place down on Laverne Road. Before you get to Oakdale. The old silver trailer, hunting place, family out of Grand Rapids used to come up and use it.

"Oh yes, now I know. She get rid of that awful thing?"

"No, she fixed it up. It's really cute now. Red and white."

"Really? Now why are we talking about her?"

I started to explain, "She saw Audrey from The Co-op having a fight with Sammy a day or two before he—oh my God, I forgot to tell you something. You have an alibi."

"What?" Bev asked.

"Sammy disappeared the day you and Nana Cole came down to Grand Rapids to pick me up."

"But they don't know when Sammy died."

"It doesn't matter. A friend spoke to him on the phone

around ten that day and that's the last anyone heard from him. People were trying to find him by about four. You were gone most of that day. How could you have been involved while you were in Grand Rapids?"

"You mean if they'd asked the right question this whole, awful day could have been avoided?"

I shrugged. "Guess so."

Chapter 13

I WOKE up the next morning thinking, "I'm a student of life." That's what Sandy Edelson said I had to accept about myself. I had no idea what she meant but it sounded cool, so I didn't mind. As long as it didn't come with another student loan, I'd accept it. In fact, I accepted it so much that I got up, took a shower, snagged some breakfast—homemade biscuits with Nana Cole's raspberry freezer jam—fed my dog, and went to the library.

The Masons Bay Library was located in a square brick building that had once been a lumbermill before the loggers cut down all the trees and everyone basically had to wait a generation and a half until new ones grew. The building was two-stories, but inside the second floor was largely open. It ringed the building, with an area large enough for a set of bookshelves and a walkway. A staircase came down to the first floor and the circulation desk. Around the edge of the building on the first floor were activity rooms. At the circulation desk, a tubby guy around thirty sat at a computer.

I was going to need help and I knew it. At UCLA, I'd done almost anything to avoid the library. It was enormous, and just because I'd seen it in like a million movies didn't mean I could find anything. Luckily, I was able to write most of my papers about TV, magazines and AOL. I did much of my research at Rite Aid.

To assist in my quest, I wore my one and only flannel shirt, pink and black squares. I added a black hoodie and black jeans. I almost looked like a local.

"Hi," I said to the tubby guy. He looked up from the computer. I took that as a good sign and continued, "So, um, I want to read back issues of the *Wyandot Eagle*."

"Okay."

"Do you have those?"

He sighed. "How far back?"

"Well, the seventies I guess."

He looked at me suspiciously. I had the feeling I was interrupting something. Like he was surfing for porn online or something.

"The nineteen seventies?"

"Yeah."

He sighed, heavily this time. I decided I needed to get him on my side, so I tried the truth. I mean, why not?

"I want to find out more about Sammy Hart. The guy who was murdered. I kind of found his body."

That perked him up. "You found his body? What was *that* like?"

Going with my gut, I said, "I only really saw his feet. But something had been chewing on his ankle."

"Oh God." Disgust and excitement mingled. "Okay, well, the thing about the *Eagle* is, we've got most of it on fiche. But... we haven't completely cataloged it. So you can't just look up where the articles are about Mr. Hart."

"You mean I'd have to sit and read every issue?"

It was a weekly newspaper but still. The seventies.

"Well," he said, then looked around the empty library as though he didn't want anyone to hear. "The morgue *is* downstairs."

The morgue was in the basement of the library? *Oh my God, this is a small town.* Keeping dead bodies below all the books—

Something in my face must have tipped him off because he

said, "No, not that morgue. The *Eagle's* morgue. A newspaper morgue."

"Oh. What is that?"

"Before technology newspapers used to keep copies of every article and photograph they published in files cross referenced by subject."

"And you have those files?"

"Yeah, we've got eight file cabinets in the basement. We've been using them to catalogue the fiche, but we're only at C."

"But you might have a file on Sammy Hart downstairs?"

"We probably do."

"Is there a way I could look at it?"

He considered for a moment, though I had no idea why. It was a library. He was supposed to give me the things I asked for. That was the whole point.

"All right. I'll go get you the file. Is Mr. Hart's the only file you want to see?"

"I think so."

"Take a seat, I'll be back in a few minutes." He pointed at a table with four chairs. "If anyone comes to the desk, tell them I'll be right back."

As he walked away, I realized the library was not quite as empty as I'd thought. Across from me, on the other side of the circulation desk, there was a row of four computers open to the public. Two of them had people in front. Guys just a little older than me. Job hunting? Then I noticed a young woman in the stacks on the second floor. Odd how they'd been invisible just a few minutes before.

When the librarian came back, he held a thick manila folder. Thicker than I'd expected.

"So, who are you?" he asked.

"Oh, my name is Henry Milch. I'm staying with my grandmother, Emma Cole."

"Okay. I'm Chad, head librarian."

"Hi Chad." That was a terrible name, he must have suffered terribly during the 2000 election fiasco.

Hanging Chad set the file down in front of me. "Please be

careful. The newsprint is old." Then he said, "I'll be right over here," meaning the circulation desk. I think he also meant that he'd be watching me.

I made myself comfortable, slipped my hoodie off and yawned. Libraries made me sleepy. I opened the file and looked at the first article. LOCALS PROTEST IRAQ WAR. It was from the October 30, 2002 issue. I quickly scanned it. The important part was, "A small group of protestors gathered in downtown Bellflower on Saturday, October 26, against the possibility of war in Iraq. Led by activist, Sammy Hart, the group joined other protests around the world."

That told me a couple of things, most important, that the file was not in any real order. I stopped and spent a few minutes carefully putting the articles in order. The oldest article was actually Sammy's birth announcement published September 15, 1948.

It said, "A son, Samuel Anthony Hart, was born to Lorenzo and Colleen Hart on Friday, September 10, 1948, at 1:42 a.m. at St. Anne's Hospital in Bellflower. Samuel weighed 7 pounds 6 ounces and measured 22 inches long at birth. Grandparents are Robert and Sylvia Beckett of Masons Bay and Antonio and Loretta Hart of Detroit."

Since the most recent article was from 2002, I went over to Hanging Chad and asked, "Not everything is in the file, right? Because there should be articles about his disappearance."

"Well, the last six weeks are always in the periodical section," he nodded toward a couple of chairs set in a square near the computers. "But, also, Marcy Wilkins has been sick. She comes in from the *Eagle* and keeps the morgue up to date. She's behind."

"Okay, um, thanks."

So, when I finished with the file I was going to need to go through the last six weeks. I mean, maybe. I knew I wasn't going to run across an article that said, so-and-so killed Sammy. I already knew most of what was in those articles so maybe I wouldn't bother. I slunk back over to the file.

After the birth announcement, there were a few mentions of

Sammy as a child, 4-H prizes, Boy Scout events. Whoever had cut the articles out in the fifties and sixties had used a lead pencil to underline his name in each of those articles. His father, Lorenzo Hart, passed away on August 8, 1969, when Sammy was around twenty-one.

Then there was nothing until the July 18, 1973 issue of the Eagle: "Samuel Hart, 24, of Coldwater was arrested for running a bawdy house in the tiny hamlet. Four others were apprehended at the same time and charged with lewd behavior and sodomy. Neighbors tipped off police after frequent visits and loud noise music came from the three-bedroom ranch house. It is believed Hart ran the establishment in his basement."

After that there were a couple of articles as Sammy was arraigned, tried and then convicted. He was sentenced to one year in prison and a five hundred dollar fine.

There was no mention of him getting out of prison. Hopefully, he wasn't in long. With good behavior it might have only ended up being a couple of months.

The next two stories were sixteen years later. One was the obituary for Colleen Beckett Hart who died on March 14, 1989. Sammy is mentioned as her son. And the other, another obituary for a Davis Turley who died on June 23, 1989, at the age of 47. Sammy Hart was mentioned as his longtime companion.

The next article, from later in 1989, took a different kind of tone than earlier write-ups. "Local gay activist Sammy Hart has donated the funds to begin an AIDS clinic in memory of his partner, Davis Turley. The clinic will be located adjacent to Morley Medical Center (formerly St. Anne's Hospital) in Bellflower and will offer testing and counseling to those impacted by AIDS."

It went on from there, but I was already reading the next headline: LOCAL AIDS CLINIC VANDALIZED. In February of 1991, the clinic's windows were broken and the wall was spray-painted with slurs. The article declined to mention what slurs, but the accompanying photo showed the words "DIE

FAGOT" scrawled on the wall. F-A-G-O-T. Bigots really did need to learn how to spell.

There were several other articles about the clinic being protested or vandalized. Each mentioned Sammy as clinic bene-factor and/or president of the board.

In 1997, there were a couple of articles about men being arrested in Big Turtle National Park for public lewdness. The article quoted local gay activist Sammy Hart, saying that the men had been lured there and entrapped by the county sheriff's office. One of the articles mentioned Sammy paying for their defense. The briefest of the articles on this subject told me that the charges against the men had been dropped.

Then I found a story from 1999, April. Just four years ago. "BELLFLOWER MAN FOUND BEATEN." A Bellflower man, 50, was found badly beaten on Bayview between Lakeside and First streets in Bellflower. The victim was located several doors down from Mr. Chips, a well-known gay bar." Obviously, whoever wrote that had never actually been to a gay bar. Someone had written Sammy's name in pencil in the margin, which seemed to defeat the purpose of not mentioning his name in the article.

There were no other articles about this. I wondered if there might be a connection to the public lewdness arrests. Sammy was beaten up a little more than a year after those charges were dropped. Was someone angry about that? Or was it just a random bashing? Maybe he got drunk at the bar and pissed someone off.

For some reason it felt important even though I didn't know why. I was out of articles to read. I could flip through the last six weeks, but I was starving and I didn't think I'd find out much that I didn't know. He disappeared. No one did anything. And then he was found. That kind of covered it.

Even though I was hungry, I sat in the chair for a long while. I felt a little stunned. Up until that morning, Sammy Hart hadn't been much more than a couple of loafered-feet in the snow. Not a real person. But now, suddenly, he felt a lot more real. He was a person with a history. A person to whom bad things had happened, and good too. But mostly bad.

My cousin. I reminded myself that Sammy was my cousin. Well, my third cousin repeatedly removed. Still, this was someone who could have been me. Well, if I was born a long, long time ago. And now he was dead. Someone had killed him. All that was left of him were a corpse and memories and newsprint.

Chapter 14

WELL, that was depressing. I really needed an Oxy or two, but I'd taken them all. Which, by the way, is the worst thing about liking drugs; they always run out. I decided I'd distract myself with something light, frivolous and preferably sweet. The mischievously named Fudge You! was two doors down from the library, so I popped in and bought a quarter pound of vanilla chocolate chip and another quarter pound of black cherry. Then I ate the fudge on the drive to Bellflower listening to Mandy Moore sing about how she had a crush on me. Believe me, eating fudge while singing along to a pop song and driving a four-speed truck is a skill. A valuable skill.

I found the Turley HIV Clinic about a block from Midland Hospital formerly Morley Medical Center formerly St. Anne's. Seriously, who can keep up? Anyway, the clinic was a squat, square brick building. I almost didn't find it because the sign was so teeny-weeny. The rainbow flag waving above the door was bigger—that's how I finally found it.

I parked at a meter, threw in a quarter—I wasn't planning on being there long—and scurried into the building. It was thirty-five degrees out and I was in a hoodie. I thought it was absurd that no one else was rushing. Or even looked cold.

Inside, I found a rather large, empty waiting room. Behind a desk at the far end of the room sat Toddy. Looking at him again,

I decided he was very good-looking. I liked his hair. It was that kind of blond that was very light on top and dark underneath. His eyes were hazy blue and his skin freshly pink. The only strike against him that I could see as I walked across the room was that he was wearing a sweater with a shawl collar. I couldn't remember what decade it was from, but it wasn't this one.

"Hi Toddy, do you remember me? Henry Milch. Mooch."

"Of course, I remember you Henry. What can I do for you?"

"Well, I wanted to ask a couple of questions."

"Are you here for an HIV test?"

"Oh God, no."

"When was the last time you were tested?"

"Last year sometime." Maybe it was two years. Who pays attention, right?

"We could do the test now. We have rapid response testing. It only takes twenty minutes."

"Thanks, but I'm here to ask questions about Sammy Hart."

"Why?"

"What?"

"Why? Why is that *your* business?"

The last thing I wanted to do was mention the reward. I mean, I'm sure he knew about it, but he didn't need to know I wanted it.

"Well, I found his body. I feel like I owe him something." I'm sure that sounded as pathetic as it felt. "He's kind of my cousin."

Nope, that was also lame.

Toddy looked me over for a moment, then stood up, saying, "Let's do the test. You can ask your questions while we wait."

He walked back to a small exam room situated behind the desk. I had no choice but to follow. I didn't want to take the test. I was sure I was fine but if I wasn't it would ruin my day and I wasn't in the mood to have my day ruined. Besides, I was sober. I would never deliberately take an HIV test while sober. I mean, that was ridiculously dumb.

The room was small, with just a built-in desk and a set of wall shelves above it. Toddy sat down in one chair and offered me the other mere inches away. On the desk, there was a sheet opened up and on it were some plastic tools that looked pretty unfamiliar.

"You can take your hoodie off," he said.

"That's okay."

Toddy put on a pair of gloves. I really wanted to get out of this. "Do you have a quota?" I asked. It would explain why he was so intent on testing me.

He chuckled. "No, I'm barely paid. It's important that everyone be tested though. Knowledge is power." Maybe that was true, I don't know. Sometimes knowledge was just depressing.

Since there didn't seem to be a way to stop this, I just went ahead and asked my first question, "Tell me about the meeting you were supposed to have with Sammy on the day he disappeared."

"It was the initial meeting for our annual fundraiser. We do a fancy-dress dinner in May. Well, usually in May. We may push it back this year due to Sammy's death."

I almost asked if there might be a connection between that meeting and his death but that seemed silly, dumb even. Instead, I asked, "So, Sammy got beat up outside Mr. Chips in ninety-nine, do you know anything about that?"

"Oh my, you have done your research. Um, gosh, he would never talk about that, but I've heard rumors."

"What rumors?"

"How many sexual partners have you had in the last year?" Toddy asked, very official.

"None of your business."

"It's for our records. Don't worry, it's anonymous. I won't tell anyone, I promise."

This was not going the way I wanted it to. "What kind of rumors?" I asked again, trying to get back on solid ground.

"Well, at first, everyone thought it was a hate crime. But

then Sammy wasn't cooperating with the sheriff. He said he just wanted it forgotten."

"If it was a hate crime he wouldn't want it forgotten," I said, thinking about the man I'd spent two hours reading about. "Do you think he knew whoever beat him up?"

"How many sex partners?"

I sighed heavily. I didn't like this game. "In the last year, I don't know. Ten, twelve. I usually notch my bed post, but I don't have it with me."

"And do you practice safer sex?"

"Sure, why not?"

"Every time?"

"Mostly. So who do you think beat Sammy up?"

"Probably whoever killed him. Don't you think?"

"But why wait four years?"

"I have no idea. I didn't kill him. You're going to feel a little prick." The last sounded rehearsed. And a little flirtatious.

"Is that a joke—ouch."

"Sorry," he said, continuing to mess around with my finger. I could tell that he had a smile on his face. He was enjoying this.

I was at a loss. I could try to think who might have beaten Sammy up, but I was likely to end up with the same kind of list I'd come up with for those who could have killed him. A long one.

If it weren't for the four-year gap I'd be completely convinced there was a connection. But the gap was there. And that meant it was entirely possible Sammy's getting beaten happened for a different reason than his getting killed.

Toddy was doing something with a piece of plastic that kind of looked like a pregnancy test—or at least what they looked like in commercials. I'd actually never seen one close up, thank God.

"Did you know more Americans will die in Michigan this year from AIDS than will die in Iraq and Afghanistan combined?"

"Are you psychic?" I asked. Seriously, how do you know numbers from the future?

"Assuming no one drops an atomic bomb on our troops, that is."

I had no idea what he expected me to do with that information. I mean, a lot of people would die of AIDS in 2003. I got it. Or did I? I thought the new drugs were taking care of all that. Wasn't it all kind of, well, over?

"Oops, here we go." He stared at the plastic stick, leaving a suspenseful pause. Finally, he looked up at me. "Negative."

"Oh. Great." I was actually very relieved. Being positive would have just made everything in my life worse. Believe it or not, I wasn't good at taking pills when I was supposed to, only when I wasn't supposed to.

"You do need to be better about safer sex. Every time. Okay?"

"Um, sure."

I sat there for a moment trying to think up what I needed to ask Toddy. There was more, I was sure, but I couldn't—

"Was Sammy HIV positive?"

"I can't share that information."

"Not professionally, I get that. But you knew Sammy socially. Did he ever mention it? At say… Mr. Chips?"

"I suppose it was common knowledge," Toddy admitted. "Yes, Sammy was HIV positive."

"Do you think he gave it to—" I stopped. Toddy was definitely *not* going to answer that question so there was no reason to even ask it. I stood up. "I should go. Thanks for the test."

When we left the exam room, he surprisingly followed me to the front door. As I reached to open it, he said, "Rupert Beckett."

"What?"

"The rumor was always that Rupert Beckett beat Sammy up in ninety-nine. Some kind of family dispute."

I was beginning to think that it was a good thing I never got invited to family reunions.

———

BEFORE I LEFT BELLFLOWER, I went by The Co-op. I wanted to find out more about this Audrey person. The building was square, flat-roofed and brick. Someone had the bright idea to paint it Mandarin orange—probably because the paint was on sale—and then add various vegetables in yellow. It was not appetizing.

I parked in the parking lot and sat in the car thinking. I'd look a lot less suspicious if I bought something. But if I brought home random food items Nana Cole would rip me a new one wanting to know why I didn't ask what she wanted. I got out my flip phone.

"This is Henry," I said, even though her landline showed my number. "I'm at The Co-op, do you want anything?"

I almost said nothing perishable because growing up in Southern California you never left food in the car. But here, in April, I could leave whatever she wanted on the front seat and in minutes it would be colder than if it were in the fridge.

"What are you doing *there*?" she asked.

"I was driving by."

"Well, I need eggs and bread and some good hamburger, about two pounds. But that's going to cost a fortune, why don't you go to Meijers?"

"Because I'm at The Co-op and I don't want to drive for another forty minutes. I'll get you what you want. Is that it?"

"Why are you in Bellflower?"

"Because I am."

"Henry, that's not an answer."

Now I wish I hadn't called at all. I could tell her I got an HIV test. It would be the truth, but she'd totally freak. I tried, "I had a doctor's appointment." It was close to the truth at least.

"What doctor? For what?"

"I think medical appointments are my own—"

"No. No Henry, they're not. What doctor?"

Fuck. I'd really screwed this up. I couldn't believe I was so stupid. Now she thought I was doctor shopping to get pills. I had to think about something that would both satisfy her and get her off my back. No to mention something she couldn't check.

"I went to a therapist, all right? And no, I'm not giving you any more information than that."

Ignoring me, she asked, "Did the doctor prescribe you anything?"

"Psychologist. They can't prescribe drugs. Happy?"

She was silent for a long time. This would probably cause me trouble down the road, but for the moment it would keep her quiet.

"Mayonnaise," she said. "Bring me mayonnaise."

And with that she hung up. I sighed heavily and climbed out of the truck. I walked across the parking lot, took a cart from the row sitting outside the door, and entered the store. Inside they were going for a warehouse feel with concrete floors and an exposed ceiling. I looked around, trying to get my bearings. The checkout lanes were right there by the door. Both cashiers were women; neither fit Audrey's description.

I pushed my cart forward, hoping she was on break. Finding myself in the enormous bulk section, I decided there was nothing there I wanted. I mean, I didn't need pounds and pounds of dried white beans, and I didn't even know what to do with almond flour. I went up and down the rows until I found the mayonnaise that Nana Cole wanted. Well, maybe wanted. There were half a dozen kinds: vegan, olive oil, safflower, free range—I had no idea what that had to do with mayonnaise— and plain old organic. I got the organic. I found the eggs and the hamburger—I could only afford a pound and skipped the bread entirely. Along the way, I also found super healthy-looking potato chips and a bag of organic cookies called No-Reos.

Then I went over and got into the checkout line. I wanted to open the bag and try one of the cookies. If they were good, I'd get another bag. Too late. It was my turn. I took my items and set them on the counter. The cashier, a woman in her fifties wearing a nametag that said ROSE, began scanning my items.

"Is Audrey here?"

"She doesn't work on Mondays or Tuesdays."

"Ah, okay. Um, do you have her number?"

"Why?"

"She's a friend."

"She's a friend and you don't have her number?"

"A new friend."

"She's married. Married women don't have *new* friends like you. That'll be nineteen seventy-one."

"Jesus Christ."

Chapter 15

BY MID-AFTERNOON, I was back in Masons Bay and walking into Bayside Bar & Grill, which was a block down from the library on the opposite side of Main Street. Inside, everything seemed to be made of heavily varnished wood: the floors, the booths, the bar itself. The walls were decorated with signs that said silly things like, I'D RATHER BE SAILING and LIFE IS BETTER WITH A CHERRY ON TOP.

Normally I would have sat at a booth, but Toddy had told me that Rupert Beckett spent most of his afternoons at the Bayside's bar. I bellied up, took my earbuds out, and ordered a Miller Genuine Draft. I can barely stand beer but, as they say, when in Rome. Or in this case, Masons Bay.

Looking around, it was clear Rupert wasn't there. Everyone was well over fifty. Not surprising I suppose. Who else could afford regular day-drinking? Sitting next to me was a man in his early sixties with a bumpy, red clown nose and flushed cheeks. I wondered if he'd gotten there that morning when the bar opened.

The barmaid was in her forties, big-breasted and slim-hipped. She wore her thick brown hair in a ponytail to supply some ballast. She put the beer in front of me and I asked for a menu. Reaching under the bar, she pulled one out.

Glancing through quickly, I decided on a blue cheese bacon

burger with an order of curly fries. I'd had almost nothing but sugar all day. I needed some meat to balance that out. After she took my order, the barmaid looked at the man next to me and asked, "You want another, Rupert?"

He did.

Rupert. His name was Rupert. Well, I figured out what was going on pretty quickly. This was Rupert Beckett *senior*. I'd been expecting Rupert *junior*. The thing was, Toddy must have meant Rupert Sr. when he sent me, so could this old man have beaten Sammy up? It was four years ago; this Rupert would have been in his late-fifties then—provided I was guessing his age correctly. Maybe he wasn't in his early sixties now. Day-drinkers age rather quickly. Maybe he was in his mid-fifties. Or even his early fifties. His son was in his mid-twenties, so somewhere in there would be about right.

As the bartender set down his new drink, I asked, "Are you Rupert Beckett?"

"Yeah. Who are you?" The chip on his shoulder was big enough to explain the way he bent over the bar. It must have been hard to carry.

"I think we're related. Distantly."

"William or Roland?"

"What?"

"Alexander Beckett had two sons. If you're a Beckett, you're related to either William or Roland. I'm on the William side. If you're on the Roland side it's a real stretch to say we're related."

"Oh. I don't know. My grandmother is Emma Cole. I'm Henry Milch. I mean, I think—"

"You're on the William side, Henry. Your grandmother is my second cousin."

"Did you know her much, growing up?"

"Kind of. She used to babysit some of my friends. Then she got married. She was pretty when she was young. I knew your great uncle better."

"My great uncle?"

"Yeah, your great uncle. Bert Sheck."

This was news to me. No one had ever mentioned him.

"From the look on your face you've never heard of him."

"Um, no, I haven't."

"Bert was in the army during Viet Nam. Went AWOL. They found him in Australia, I think."

"I have relatives in Australia?"

"They found him dead."

Well, that was disappointing. I'd watched *The Adventures of Priscilla* about a million times. I wouldn't have minded seeing the outback in person. Particularly if I had a couch to crash on, which now I guess I didn't.

"Your grandmother doesn't talk much about the family?"

"No. She doesn't. I mean, I just found out we're related to Sammy Hart. Which is weird because I found his body."

"Did you? I'm jealous."

"Jealous. What do you mean you're jealous?"

"Let's say I wasn't close to my cousin. I wouldn't have minded spitting on his corpse."

"I guess you didn't like him much. Why not?"

"Aside from the fact that he was a pervert?"

"Yeah, aside from that." I would never have put up with that in L.A., I mean, I wouldn't have punched him or anything... But I would have called him a bigot or an asshole or something and then very pointedly stormed off. In fact, there was one time—

"He had no family loyalty," Rupert said. "After my aunt died, my boy and I wanted to develop that land of hers on Goose Lake, but Sammy wouldn't sell it to us."

Which might have had something to do with them calling him a pervert, I was tempted to point out.

"That why you beat him up in ninety-nine?"

He turned and looked me full on. Then he broke into a creepy smile. "I guess the statue of limitations has run out on that one. Yeah, I beat him up. Enjoyed it too."

The barmaid slipped my burger in front of me. You'd think I'd have trouble eating it sitting there next to someone like Rupert Beckett.

But I didn't.

———

WHEN I GOT BACK to Nana Cole's the wind was howling, coming in off the lake like a train. Zipping my hoodie up to my chin, I grabbed the groceries and got out of the truck. I called for Reilly a few times, but he didn't come. I wasn't sure if he could hear me over the barreling wind. Giving up, I went into the house through the kitchen door.

Nana Cole sat at the table cleaning her hunting rifle and listening to the radio while something cooked on the stove. I didn't recognize the show she was listening to—a couple of men were gleefully talking about the war and how we were crushing al Qaeda, which you knew wasn't exactly happening if you read a paper or watched a legitimate news channel.

"You're cleaning your rifle," I said. I didn't consider it a good sign. About two weeks after I got there she'd gone out and shot some rabbits and then made a stew. I'd refused to eat it.

"Yup, wild turkey season. Two weeks."

"Oh goodie."

"It's delicious. You'll see." She correctly interpreted my silence, saying, "You want a bologna sandwich then."

"Is it bologna season?" I teased. Of course, we both knew that bologna was made of God knows what and should be less appetizing than a wild turkey, but somehow wasn't.

I stood there stiffly, groceries still hand, watching her. "Where do you keep that thing?"

She looked up at me, stopped what she was doing, and chewed her lip.

"It's okay. You can tell me where you keep the rifle. I *didn't* try to kill myself no matter what my mother said. I can't believe you picked now to start believing her."

"I don't believe her, but even a broken clock is right twice a day."

I sighed heavily and said, "Oh my God."

"I keep it in the workshop. There's a gun case in there. Which you'd know if you took an interest."

"Thank you. I appreciate your believing me."

"I don't believe you. I just think if you're going to kill yourself it's not going to matter if I hide the gun, you'll find some way to do it. If you decide to use my rifle go right ahead. I won't feel guilty. Don't do it in the house though, I don't want the mess."

I stood there, mouth hanging open. I wasn't sure how to react to what she'd just said. Was she saying she didn't care if I killed myself? It didn't sound like that, except it kind of did. Just then, Reilly bounded into the room and jumped on me, and then sniffed me a few times.

"He stinks," Nana Cole said. At first, I wasn't sure which of us she meant. "If he's going to be in the house you need to give him a bath."

"Um, sure, okay," I said, finally putting the groceries on the counter. Cleaning the dog gave me an excuse to get out of the room and away from the cleaning of weapons. "Do we have any dog shampoo?"

"People shampoo won't kill him."

"Okay."

I was pretty sure there was a reason dog shampoo existed, other than to make the manufacturer money. But taking Reilly to the groomer the month before had nearly bankrupted me. Even the idea of going near the pet store seemed like a really bad idea.

"I'm making boiled dinner."

"I had a burger at Bayside. I'm not hungry."

"What were you doing at Bayside?"

"Six weeks ago you were all up in my grill because I didn't leave my room. Can't you just be happy I'm going places?"

"What do you mean 'grill?' What are you talking about?"

I rolled my eyes and left the room, calling Reilly to come with me. We went upstairs to my bedroom. The dog jumped on the bed, thinking we were going to hang out. Since I'd come with just one suitcase, I didn't have a lot of clothes that would qualify as crappy enough to wash the dog in. I changed into pajama bottoms and a T-shirt. They were at least easily washed. Then I led Reilly to the bathroom.

Nana Cole's bathroom was nice, but old. She had a claw-foot bathtub with recent tile stuck up all around it. The bathtub was great because it was deep, but that was also kind of a problem when you were trying to get a seventy-pound lab mix to jump into it.

I'd closed the door so that Reilly was trapped in there with me. I plugged the drain with the rubber stopper and turned on the water, making sure it was tepid. He was giving me a suspicious look. I wasn't sure whether it was the idea of a bath he didn't like or my obvious lack of experience.

"It'll be over quickly," I promised him.

As you entered the large room, there was a cabinet that acted as a linen closet. I opened it and looked at the different kinds of shampoo Nana Cole had on hand. There were three bottles of a generic brand in lavender. She liked to buy things in bulk.

There was also a half empty bottle of baby shampoo. I had no idea why she had it. It wasn't forty-five-years-old, so she hadn't used it on my mother. It also wasn't twenty-four-years old, so it hadn't been used on me.

It was only a couple of years old. Maybe it was for my grandfather. He'd been sick a long time. Maybe she'd had to wash his hair and didn't want to get stingy soap in his eyes? Anyway, that seemed like the best one to use on Reilly. A dog that smelled like lavender didn't seem like a good idea.

When the bathtub was half-full, I turned off the water. I put some shampoo in and swished it around. My strategy was simply to get as much soap and water on the dog as I could and hope for the best. I scooped Reilly up, like a cowboy picking up a calf, and set him into the tub. With cupped hands, I tried to get him wet, having to stop every few scoops to block him from getting out. Clearly, he was not enjoying the bath.

Once I got him soaped up, I realized I should have brought something to rinse him off with, a bowl or something. The only thing handy in the bathroom was the rinse cup from the vanity. I grabbed it and started trying to rinse off the very large dog. He, however, had better ideas. He gave himself a mighty shake and covered me in doggy, soapy, droplets. That was when I gave up and pulled out the plug. He was out of the bathtub in a flash and I spent a good five minutes trying to towel dry him. He wasn't crazy about that either.

Eventually, I gave up trying to towel him off and simply let the whimpering dog run around wet, shaking water everywhere.

Now what? I had the whole night ahead of me with nothing to do. That's when I remembered I was out of Oxy. I went directly to my bedroom and found my flip phone. Scanning through the numbers, I found Opal's and clicked on it. I should have changed my clothes first; my T-shirt and pajama bottoms were so wet they clung to me. I was getting a chill, but I had something to—

"Hello?"

"Hey, this is Henry," I said, trying to sound casual.

"Yeah, I know. It's the twenty-first century. I have Caller ID, I know who's calling. Remember?"

"So, you mentioned some guy who sells pot. Can you give me his name?"

"Why do you need pot?" she asked.

That was a ridiculous question. No one *needed* pot, and everyone *needed* pot. I mean, there were many highs I preferred, but marijuana was a perfect fallback position. When all else fails, smoke a doobie.

I decided to give Opal the kind of answer she deserved. "My grandmother has glaucoma."

"No, she doesn't."

"Why ask questions if you're not going to believe the answers?" I asked.

"You never know, you might have told me the truth."

"Just tell me the guy's name."

"Ronnie Sheck."

"Does he live at the Sheck farm?"

"No, he's not one of those Shecks."

For some reason, the phrase *different finger, same hand* came to mind. Was this why Nana Cole was so attached to the idea? Because everyone up here was connected but not connected at the same time?

"You're not a Sheck, are you?"

"No."

"A Beckett?"

"No."

"Mason?"

"My mother moved up from Grand Rapids after she divorced my father. I was five. I'm not related to anyone—except my mother—for over a hundred and fifty miles. Okay?"

"So, can I have his number?"

"No."

"What do you mean, no?"

"It doesn't work that way."

"How does it work?"

"You have to be recommended by someone he knows. Let me call him and I'll call you back."

She hung up on me. I took the time to change into a pair of jeans and a teal cashmere sweater from Banana Republic. I wondered if I had time to go back and clean up the bathroom. I really needed to before Nana Cole saw it. She'd have a cow if she—

My phone rang. Opal.

"Yeah?"

"15 Queens Way Court. It's on Turtle Highway before you get to Coldwater."

I vaguely knew where that was.

"How late can I go? Like, what are his hours?"

"Are you kidding me? He's not a convenience store."

Then she hung up on me, I spent a few minutes mopping the bathroom up and then I went downstairs to watch *JAG* with my grandmother.

Chapter 16

IN MY EXPERIENCE, drug dealers never live in nice places. Which doesn't make sense since it's like a kazillion dollar business. But it does explain why Ronnie lived in Queens Way Mobile Home Park, which had not been immediately apparent from the address Opal had given me. I drove by it twice until I saw Queens Way on the sign out front.

The park was small with only one street that ran around in a perfect square. Everyone who lived in the park lived on Queens Way Court. Number 15 was a sharp-edged, uninspired singlewide from the seventies with a pop-out attached to the living room. I parked in front of it, went up to the door and knocked.

It was still glacially cold, thirty degrees if we were lucky. It was like living in a giant refrigerator all the time. The fact that it was officially spring seemed like a cruel joke. Like having a boyfriend but never getting laid.

The door opened. A short, scrawny kid stood there. Well, he looked like a kid of about fifteen, but when you examined him closely he was clearly around thirty. Casting directors in Hollywood would have adored him. He could play high school seniors for most of his life.

"Are you Ronnie?"

He grunted and walked away from the door, leaving it open.

I stepped inside, closing the door behind me. The walls were the first thing I noticed: They were peach with a confetti pattern. From where I stood I could see into the kitchen, which had been painted in three sherbet shades of orange that didn't quite match the peach confetti walls.

The living room/dining room area was filled with furniture: a round, wooden table that sat six; a giant padded sofa; three black leather reclining chairs; a coffee table—complete with three bongs and various other paraphernalia; a giant television, playing some weird sci-fi mess with Tom Cruise; and a bookcase stuffed with half of the DVDs ever released. Probably not the good half.

On the sofa and in one of the recliners were four guys of various ages and sizes, all totally baked. From the smell of the place they probably hadn't taken a break in like five years. Standing in the middle of the room, holding a bag of yellow pills, was Sammy's friend, Richard. We stared at each other.

"Where did you park?" Ronnie asked.

"Just in front."

"No, no, no. Next time don't do that. You have to park out on Turtle Highway. The people who run the park get really pissy about it."

"I'm going to take off," Richard said quietly.

"Oh sure, yeah, no worries," Ronnie replied.

"You were going to give me twenty in change."

"Oh yeah, yeah, yeah." He curled over and took a crinkled mess of bills out of his jeans pocket. He picked out two tens.

"Okay, thanks."

Then Richard walked by me on his way out. He had a drug problem. Wait, no, I shouldn't assume that. People assumed that about me and I just liked to party. So maybe Richard just liked to party now and then. For all I knew that little baggie of pills would last him a year. Although, probably not.

The door thwacked shut. I looked at Ronnie and said, "Opal sent me."

"Yup, yup, yup, you look just like she said you would."

I wasn't sure whether to be offended by that or not. "So, I

want to buy a little weed and, like, some pills since, I noticed you have those too."

I tried to be really casual about the whole thing, if I acted too interested he'd jack the price.

"I have pills, yeah."

"Okay, so I'd like an eighth."

"That's fifty."

"And Oxy?"

"I've got some 10s. I can let you have ten for seventy-five."

"I've only got forty left after the eighth." I was tempted to cancel the eighth entirely.

"I'll give you four then."

"Five. New customer discount."

He looked me over. I could tell he was trying to figure out how often I'd be back. How much of a discount I'd want each time. And whether I was generally more or less annoying than his other clients.

"Sure. Five for forty. You got it."

He busied himself putting together my order. I looked at the other guys in the room. They'd barely taken their eyes off the TV. I'd gone to see the movie in the theater but hadn't managed to stay awake through the whole thing. Mostly what I remembered was that it was blue. Everything in the movie was some shade of blue. Like the future was blue. Even Tom Cruise was blue.

Ronnie held out one plastic baggie with a couple buds of marijuana in it and another with my five precious pills. In exchange, I handed him all my cash.

"Pleasure," he said.

"Yeah, see ya," I said, and let myself out.

Driving back to Nana Cole's, I calculated how long the pills would last. Not long. If I was really careful and remembered to take them only on an empty stomach… who was I kidding. As soon as I took one I'd take another. So I had enough to get high twice. And that was disappointing.

I got paid in a little less than a week, but my part-time job was not going to support my part-time drug habit. And that brought me back to the reward. I had to get the reward. I had to get out of Wyandot County and back to L.A. where I could get a shitty job that paid more than the shitty job I had here. Ack, life was hard.

The asshole behind me had their lights on bright. I futzed with the rearview mirror because they were making me squint. And seriously, why didn't they just pass me? The way people drove around here. I mean, I was going five miles over the 45 mile an hour speed limit. How fast did he want to go?

Whoever it was seemed to get even closer, so I sped up a little. Big Turtle Highway was not my idea of a highway, trust me. My idea of a highway had at least three lanes coming and going. This was one lane on each side and not much of a shoulder. And dark. Dark as shit. Occasionally, there would be a house, a nursery, a John Deere dealership. Up ahead, I could see the lights of a no-name gas station I'd passed. Three self-pay pumps, a minimart and a brightly lit kind of roof hanging over everything.

Part of me was always thinking, where am I? I mean, seriously, where was I? I looked up a few things on Yahoo! after I arrived: Wyandot County had 15,342 people—probably 15,343 since I hadn't been counted—spread over 1,954 square miles. East Hollywood, the grungy, not very popular, ultimately pretty fabulous, part of Hollywood where I lived with Vinnie, had more than 22,000 people per square mile. More people in a mile than in this entire freaking county. That little fact goes a long way toward explaining my culture shock.

This guy would not get off my ass. I squinted and tried to figure out what kind of car it was, but all I could see was that it was big, tall, some kind of SUV maybe or a truck. I decided I'd pull off into the gas station coming up and let the guy pass me.

I checked the tank. I should probably go ahead and get gas too. But, wait, I'd just spent all my money. I tried to remember if I had any credit cards that still worked. There was one VISA that might have a couple hundred—wait, should I get a cash advance on that while I still could? I put the blinker on. I mean just because he was an ass—

The SUV, or whatever it was, started to pass me. Thank God. I wanted to be rid—in the corner of my eye I could see the grayish hood and then everything went wrong. The SUV slammed into me. The F-150 veered to the left a little, like I was going to end up in front of this guy, I spun the wheel trying to correct and bounced over what was probably a curb. I was practically standing on the clutch and the brake, but the truck was still speeding forward, the other vehicle having propelled it forward. I was barreling across the gas station lot heading right toward the furthest pump.

No! My mind was screaming... I spun the wheel, letting up on the brake to try and get some control. I downshifted as I just missed the pump. That left me heading right for an old Pontiac Fiero with a FOR SALE sign in its window.

With a giant thud, I hit the car and flew forward. The shoulder belt stopped me, but my face jerked downward and smacked the steering wheel hard. Then I bounced back and hit my head against the headrest. Meanwhile, my foot slipped off the brake and got jammed between it and the gas pedal, totally messing up my ankle. I'd stopped though. And I hadn't taken out a gas pump.

Holy shit! Was this going to happen every time I bought a little weed?

———

I REALLY DIDN'T NEED an ambulance. I could have, maybe, I don't know, found another way to get to the hospital, but the guy who worked in the minimart ran out to see what had happened. At first, he was more concerned about the Fiero—he seemed to think it was some kind of classic—but then, given the massive amounts of blood coming out of my nose, he went back inside and called an ambulance.

Remarkably, I was sober. I'd been in a car crash and I was completely sober. I started laughing about that, making the minimart guy stare at me like I was nuts. I was probably in shock. I mean, I know I was in shock. I'd just run into a Pontiac Fiero. Who wouldn't be in shock?

Then I started worrying what to do with my pot and pills. I mean, I'd put them in the inside pocket of my puffer jacket. No one would look there. I was sober, and the accident wasn't my fault. No one was going to search me. Thank God.

Right before the ambulance arrived, I decided I had to get out of the truck. I hadn't smoked any marijuana at Ronnie Sheck's, but the place reeked. I hoped I didn't smell of it. I wanted to stand in the fresh air for a minute or two. That didn't go so well. My right ankle was completely jacked up.

So was the Fiero. I hadn't actually hit it as much as drove over half of it. The F-150 looked remarkably okay. It was built like a tank. It certainly drove like one. Well, it looked okay until I stood back and took a good look at the scratches from the SUV and noticed that the front of the truck now tilted upward at a ten-degree angle.

That's when the ambulance arrived, which was good because I was close to passing out. I wasn't really in a lot of pain, not yet, I knew I would be though. The ambulance was red, with the front of a van stuck onto a big box. Its lights were flashing. A stocky, well-built EMT jumped out of the passenger side and came over.

"Hi, I'm Mike. You the driver?"

"Uh-huh."

"What's your name?"

"Henry, but people call me Mooch."

"What's your last name, Henry?"

"Milch."

The other EMT, also muscular—*Did they go on gym dates together?*—was just walking over. He'd opened the back of the ambulance and pushed a gurney.

"Henry, we're going to help you onto the gurney now."

"I can do it," I said, hopping over on one foot.

"That's okay. It's better if we do it."

The two guys lifted me up and laid me down on the gurney.

The movement made my stomach flip, and I immediately rolled over and puked on the ground next to the gurney.

"Okay," said one of them, I didn't know which. "So, is all the blood from your nose?"

"What?" I hadn't—*Oh my God!*

"Does your stomach hurt? Did you hurt it in the crash?"

"I don't think so."

One of them took off my jacket and lifted my sweater, while the other wiped the blood off my face. Cold hands were feeling around my stomach.

"So, what happened?"

"Someone ran me off the road."

"Does this hurt?"

"Tickles."

"Okay, well that's good, tickling is good."

"Someone ran me off the road," I said again. I wasn't quite sure I believed it.

"Let's get you into the ambulance, Henry."

I don't remember a whole lot about the ride to the hospital except that it was really fast. I never could have gotten there that fast. But then I suppose flashing lights and knowing where you were really saved travel time. At some point, one of the EMTs put some cotton up my bloody nose, which was much more painful than it sounds.

I kind of remember being taken out of the back of the ambulance and delivered like a package to the ER. It was quiet, creepy quiet. It had to be after midnight by then. I didn't see any other patients, so it shouldn't have surprised me that I started getting a lot of attention right away. Still, in L.A. you only got treated quickly if you were on death's door.

They moved me from the gurney to a bed in a curtained-off area. I was left there alone for only a moment. Then the doctor came in. He turned out to be what my friend Vinnie would have called hunk-a-licious. Tall, auburn-haired, blue-eyed. I almost took out my phone to call Vinnie and gossip about him. He'd be so jealous—Vinnie, I mean. I was meeting a hot doctor.

Well, he wouldn't be jealous of the broken nose or the messed-up ankle.

"I'm Dr. Stewart. Tell me what happened to you?"

"I got run off the road and smashed into a used car."

"Run off the road by a car or a deer?"

"Car! And it was deliberate. Someone was trying to kill me."

"Uh-huh."

No one believed me. It was getting annoying. There was a nurse in the room doing stuff. I barely noticed her. She was young and cute but not my type. Dr. Stewart said to her, "Find out if the rescue guys have called the sheriff yet."

He turned back and smiled at me. I wasn't sure that meant he believed me, but at least I wasn't being ignored. Leaning in close, he carefully touched my nose. "It's broken. I'm going to need to set it."

I hope he meant he was doing that after he gave me some pain meds.

"Did the airbag do that?"

"Steering wheel. Ford truck. 1985."

"Oh yeah, that makes more sense." He looked closely at my nose, touching it gently. We're going to need to change this packing."

"Already?" Actually, what I said was "Alweady?"—but let's not even go there.

Dr. Stewart rested one hand on my shoulder, which I was extremely aware of, while the other looked through my hair. His fingers pressed gently into my scalp, particularly around the back. I tried to think of something flirtatious to say about his running his fingers through my hair, but my thoughts weren't coming together.

"Did you hit your head? The back I mean."

"I don't know. I mean, I don't think so."

"Any tenderness?"

"No."

"Can you lie back for me?"

Could I ever! Okay, maybe I'm weird but, despite my nose and messed-up ankle and possible internal injuries, I was having dirty thoughts about my doctor at the rate of two per minute. He eased me back onto the table. Gently, ever so gently. Then he felt around my stomach much more extensively than the EMT had. It was starting to get tender from all the poking and prodding. Didn't matter, I never wanted him to stop.

"You're going to have a bad bruise tomorrow. Right along here." He touched me in two spots, indicating it would be a diagonal bruise where the seat belt had grabbed me. "But I'm not feeling anything to be concerned about."

My lack of a six-pack was sometimes concerning, I thought, and it would have made a good joke except now I felt too shy to use it. All I said was, "Okay."

Dr. Stewart moved down to my feet. He took off my right boot, which caused pain to shoot everywhere. I whimpered.

"That hurt?"

"Uh, yes."

He took off my left boot. That was fine. Or at least better. He rolled my socks off. Then took a good look at my feet and ankles, touching me gently a few times. He moved my left foot around and it wasn't too bad. Then he did the same with my right and I kind of screamed.

"Okay, we're going to need an X-ray."

Broken! My ankle was broken! How was I going to find Sammy's killer with a broken ankle? How was I going to get the reward and get out of Wyandot County?

"You think it's broken?" I said, hoping he'd contradict me.

"It may just be a sprain."

A sprain. Thank God. That was so much better. I'd be fine in a day or two.

"Don't get too excited, though. Sometimes a sprain is worse than a break."

Then he left me alone. I decided I didn't like him. I didn't care how sexy he was. Worse than a break. Seriously?

Chapter 17

DETECTIVE LEHMANN SHOWED up after I'd had my X-rays. Without a 'hello' or 'how are you?'—which would have been appropriate in an ER—he asked, "What happened?"

"I got run off the road."

"Yes, I understand that's what you've been telling people."

"You don't believe me?"

"There's gray paint on your truck. And the other driver didn't stop. So, yeah, I believe you. Tell me what happened."

"I was driving along Big Turtle Highway, minding my own business, when this guy or someone started tailgating me really bad."

"Where were you coming from?"

Shit. Shit. Shit. I couldn't tell him the truth. He probably knew exactly who Ronnie Sheck was and why I'd gone there. I could say I'd gone to see Opal, but I had no idea where she lived. Plus there was the problem of it being late. What was open—

"I was at Meijer over in Traverse."

He glanced around looking for a bag. He'd looked in my truck. There was no grocery bag there.

"You were at Meijers?" he asked, adding the 's' the way locals did. "What'd you buy?"

"Nothing. They didn't have what I wanted."

"It's a big place. They have a lot of things."

"I needed underwear. They don't carry Calvin Klein." Any fool would know they didn't carry that brand at Meijer. I would never have gone there looking for that. It was obvious Lehmann knew that. He let it pass though.

"So you were driving along and being tailgated. Then what?"

"I decided to pull over into the gas station and get out of the way. I put the blinker on and the other vehicle pulled around me, then bumped me and I went flying through the gas station. I almost hit one of the pumps. I did hit a Pontiac Fiero."

"Yes, I saw that."

They were trying to kill me. Were they trying to kill me? Were they trying to send me off into the pumps? Or had it been an accident and they saw what they'd done so they ran?

"Do you remember anything about the other vehicle?"

"It was an SUV or a truck. But they had their brights on so I couldn't really see it."

"It was gray whatever it was."

"It was?"

"Yes, I told you, there's gray paint on the side of your truck." He was giving me a dubious look.

"Oh great. So we can figure out what kind of car it was?"

"No, not really."

"No?" I was sure I saw that on TV.

"If we find the vehicle we can match the paint."

"But—"

"Even if there *were* a database somewhere of every kind of paint ever put on every kind of car, it wouldn't be cost effective to use that kind of forensics as an investigative tool. Knowing that you were pushed off the road by one of a hundred thousand Chevy Blazers registered in this and nearby states doesn't narrow things down."

"But what difference does it make after you figure out who did it?"

"Forensics are most important at trial. Once we know who did something we have to prove it. That's where forensics comes in."

I wasn't sure, but I think he was telling me that if they found the car that ran me off the road then they could find the car that ran me off the road. Kind of a catch-22 thingy.

"All right, well, thank you," I said, although what I was thanking him for I certainly didn't know.

"Did anyone know you'd be driving that way?"

"I don't think so," I said quickly. Opal knew, but I wasn't going to mention that since it led right to the real purpose of my trip.

"Did you do anything to antagonize the other driver?"

"You mean was it like… road rage?" Being from L.A. I was familiar with the idea. "Um, no, no, I don't think so."

"Do you have any reason to think you're being followed?"

"Followed—?"

"Do you know of anyone who'd want to hurt you?"

"Well—"

"Well, what?"

Since someone had tried to kill me, I should at least tell the detective some of the truth. "I'm trying to get the reward for finding Sammy Hart's killer. I asked a lot of questions yesterday. Maybe I made someone nervous."

"Tell me everyone you talked to."

I told him everything I'd done, everywhere I'd gone, and who I'd talked to. Leaving out Opal and Ronnie Sheck, of course. He seemed to get angrier and angrier as I went along. When I was done he said, "You need to stop all of this."

"But the reward—I need—"

"You're not going to get the reward. Trust me, no one ever gets the reward."

"That doesn't seem fair."

"*You* think it's not fair? We've gotten almost a thousand phone calls, people with 'tips' they hope will get them the reward. We have to check out each tip, no matter how stupid."

"That sounds like a lot of work," I said lamely.

"You think?" He sighed heavily. "Look, go home and stay there. If you let Sammy's killer think they've scared you off, you'll be fine."

My mind was scrambling, trying to find a way to salvage the situation. Wait a minute. If the killer was trying to scare me off, then the last thing in the world I should do is stop. I was getting close. I didn't tell Detective Lehmann that though. It just wasn't a good idea.

"I guess you're right," I said, just as Dr. Stewart came back in.

"Am I interrupting?" he asked.

"No, we're finished," Lehmann said. To me he added, "Come in and write out a statement in a few days. No rush." Then he left without a goodbye.

The doctor smiled at me. I wondered if he put himself through medical school doing toothpaste commercials. "Your X-rays look good. No broken bones."

"Okay, that's good."

"You do have a bad sprain though. Level two, possibly level three."

That didn't mean anything to me.

"We're going to wrap your ankle up tight and give you a pair of crutches. Have you ever used crutches before?"

"Once. At Halloween. My costume was Ashton Crutches."

That made him smile. "Yeah, well, you're going to need to be careful. A Halloween party is not long enough to really get the hang of them."

"You've obviously never been to L.A."

"I went to medical school there."

"Oh." Well, that was embarrassing. "How long will I be on crutches?"

"That depends. You need to see your regular doctor. He may want to put you in a walking boot."

"Well, at least we're done with snow and ice."

"You have no idea where you are, do you?"

IN L.A., there were at least five people I could call at four in the morning and ask them to come and get me. Well, three. Two had stopped speaking to me. In Michigan, there was really only one person I could call, and she was the last person in the world I wanted to call. But I had no choice.

The Escalade pulled up to the ER entrance about quarter to five. I crutched my way out. Dr. Stewart had given me a sample pack of Percocet and a prescription for ten Oxy. I'd taken one of the Percs, so I was comfortable and calm enough to manage the crutches. The rest of it I'd tucked into the inner pocket of my puffer jacket with the rest of my stash.

"Where were you? I woke up and you were gone?" Nana Cole asked when I carefully climbed into the SUV.

"That's the part you think is important? Someone tried to kill me."

"Oh, don't be ridiculous. Who would want to kill you?"

"Detective Lehmann is taking paint scrapings off the truck in case we find the person who drove me off the road," I said.

"I'm sure that was an accident. Our neighbors aren't criminals. This isn't L.A."

"Nana, if it were an accident, which it wasn't, they still drove away. That makes it a hit-and-run. That's a crime."

She was quiet a moment. "It's very likely they'll turn themselves in tomorrow. People are like that here. Once they've thought better of their behavior, they admit what they've done. Were you high?"

"No, I wasn't high. You really want to blame this on me, don't you?"

"You haven't told me where you were."

"I was with Opal, all right?"

"Is she your girlfriend?"

"No, we're just hanging out."

"I don't know what that means? Does that mean dating? Are you dating her?"

"I guess you'd call it that. If you have to call it something."

"Then she should come to dinner. Does she go to church? I

mean, she doesn't come to my church, but there are other churches…"

"What do you mean she doesn't go to your church? She was at the pancake supper."

"I've never seen her on Sunday."

I was so tempted to tell her Opal wasn't there on Sundays because she was Jewish or, worse, Muslim, but I'd told enough lies for one conversation. Of course, I didn't want her to know about the reward and my trying to get it. She and my mother were so convinced my being there was somehow 'good' for me that I didn't want her to know I was trying to find my own way out.

I mean, I don't know what they expected to happen. Did they think I was going to stay forever? Did they think I was going to be a Michigander now?

No, that wasn't going to happen. I was getting out of there and going back to L.A. I just needed the money—shit, oh shit, oh shit, now I had *another* hospital bill. I had enough experience with hospitals to know they were probably going to charge me at least ten dollars a minute. Seriously, it cost money to just sit in the ER. How was I going to pay for this? I hadn't figured out how to pay my first hospital bill.

Oh, well. I shouldn't change my plans. I'd figure out how to pay for everything once I got back to L.A. Maybe I could go on a game show? I mean, at that particular moment I'd have been thrilled if all I got was a lovely parting gift.

When I struggled out of the Escalade—nearly falling on my face—Reilly came running. I froze. It was not a good idea for him to jump on me. I leaned against the side of the SUV and tried to keep him on the ground. I tried the move Bev had made —holding my hand flat. It didn't work. I ended up petting his head, it was ice cold.

"Did you leave him out all night?"

As she walked up to the house, Nana Cole said, "If you want to decide how the dog is taken care of you're going to have to be here to do it."

I nearly growled at her. That was completely unfair. I was running a personal errand that should only have taken forty-five minutes. Tops. Yes, it ended up taking almost seven hours, but none of that was my fault.

I mean, was it?

Chapter 18

AS MUCH AS I wanted to, I didn't go right to sleep. I had something I really had to take care of, so I went up to my room and played some Warcraft, numbly grinding a Paladin. The game worked better in off-hours anyway. At 6:30 I realized I was going to pass out soon, so I had to make the phone call, even though it was still early.

"What the fuck?" Opal said when she answered.

"I need a favor."

"Of course, you need a favor. That's the only reason you'd call me."

"It's not the only reason—" It was, kind of.

"What's wrong with you? You sound like you have a cold." The packing up my nose.

"Someone tried to kill me last night."

"What? Someone 'twied' to kill you? By giving you a head cold?"

"It's not funny." It was a little.

"I thought you were going over to see Ronnie Sheck. Don't listen to what they say. Those boys are harmless. They're too baked to hurt anyone."

"On the way back, someone drove me off the road."

"Oh wow. That sucks. Why are you—What does that have to do with me?"

"I didn't want my grandmother to know where I was—"

"Buying drugs."

"Yes, that. I told her I was with you. She kind of thinks we're a thing."

"I thought you didn't want to have sex with me?"

"I don't want to have sex with you. I want to have pretend sex with you."

"Closet case."

"Dyke."

"I'm not a dyke. I'm bi."

"Is that a hair you can split around here?"

She was silent.

"So, you think she's going to call me up and give me a pop quiz on our love affair?"

"God, I hope not. You may have to come to dinner though."

She burst out laughing.

"What's so funny?"

"This is like an Adam Sandler movie."

"Nooooo, it's not. Those movies suck. My life doesn't suck." Actually, my life did suck. I just hoped it sucked in a better way than an Adam Sandler movie.

"I like his movies," she said.

"You would."

"Do you need me to tell anymore lies for you? Or can I go back to bed?"

"Fuck you."

"Fuck you back."

I hung up on her or she hung up on me, I'm not sure which. Then I lay down on the bed. Reilly climbed up and nuzzled in alongside me. I needed to make a plan. To that end, I made a mental inventory: I had five Oxys and 4 Percs plus the prescription for ten more Oxy. That made a nice little stash. I wanted to make it last. Dr. Stewart had said I could take one or two of the Percs at a time and one or two of the Oxy when I got those from the pharmacy. But I didn't want to do things that way. I would take one pill every four hours, maybe even a half a one. Seriously, the last thing I was going to use a pain pill for was—

Nine hours later I woke up. It was four in the afternoon. Reilly was still next to me. Had he been there the whole time? He must need to go out. Desperately.

At some point, someone—presumably Nana Cole—had come in, put my ankle onto two pillows and placed a cold pack on top of it. I tried to sit up in bed. It was challenging. Digging my elbows into the mattress, I managed to sit up. The bruise on my belly must have come in full, because even the T-shirt laying against my skin seemed to hurt. The cold pack fell off my ankle and onto the floor. I don't think it was cold anymore.

My face hurt. God, my face hurt. My nose was still stuffed with packing. I wanted to take it out. It made me feel edgy just being up there, but they'd said I should wait and have my doctor take it out. Which reminded me, I needed to make an appointment. And, I needed to find a doctor to make an appointment with.

Standing up on my good foot, I reached for my crutches and hobbled out into the hallway. I made Reilly get in front of me. Yes, he needed to go out—and I also really, really need a pill. Unfortunately, they were downstairs in my puffer coat. Somehow, I needed to do both things at once.

Holding my crutches in one hand, I hopped on one foot down the stairs. Every time I accidentally tapped my foot on a carpeted stair or jostled it a bit too much it sent a bolt of pain right through me. I was grateful when I reached the first floor, I would have gotten down and kissed the floor if it had been remotely possible.

I crutched my way into the kitchen. Nana Cole stood by the stove. I leaned my crutches up against the wall and tried to put on my coat. It didn't go well. I almost fell down twice.

"Just open the door for Reilly. He knows what to do all by himself." I didn't want to do that, but it made sense. For one thing, it's not how I wanted to treat the dog. For another, I wanted to take a pill—and I could do that outside.

"That's okay, I can do it." I'd found one of the armholes, but the other was evading me.

"Let Reilly out. You can call him back in half an hour. He should be done with his business by then."

"Yes, but—"

"Stop being stubborn. Let the dog out and come sit down. You need to elevate your ankle."

I couldn't see a way out of this, so I put my jacket back on its hook, opened the door and watched Reilly bolt out with not even a backward glance at me. I closed the door and hopped over to the table. Part of me wanted to go back upstairs and ignore Nana Cole for the rest of my life, but I wasn't ready to face the stairs again. Plus, with the truck out of commission I was going to need to get rides from her. I sat down, put my ankle up on the chair next to me, and asked, "Is the truck totaled?"

"Not if I have anything to say about it. It's a damn good truck."

It was probably totaled. It couldn't possibly be worth more than the cost to fix it. It was ancient.

"I'm sorry about your truck."

"I don't think anyone was trying to kill you, but I do think it was an accident. Detective Lehmann called. He thinks it was an accident too."

"Well, I'm glad everyone who wasn't actually there has figured this out."

She ignored that, stirred whatever it was she was making, then asked me, "How do you feel?"

"Crappy."

"You look bad. Your eyes are going to be pitch black by tomorrow." She picked something up off the counter and came over with a glass of water in hand. In front of me, she laid three pills and offered me the water.

"What is that?"

"Extra Strength Tylenol. You look like you could use it."

"It's useless."

"Did you get something stronger from the doctor?"

154

"No. Remember, you pinned a note to my winter coat that said DRUG ADDICT."

"I don't know what that's supposed to mean. Your mother asked me to take care of you. That's what I'm doing."

"I'm twenty-freaking-four-years-old. I don't need to be taken care of."

"Believe it or not that's crossed my mind."

She set the glass down on the table, slammed might be a better word, and then went back over to the stove. She stirred angrily for a bit while I wondered when she might leave the room so I could get to my coat.

"I need to call Bev," I said.

"I already did. I told her you won't be available for a week or two."

A week or two? I didn't mind the time off from The Conservancy, but I couldn't wait that long to find Sammy's killer. I wanted the reward, I *needed* the reward.

"I'll be better tomorrow," I said.

"Well, I guess we'll see, won't we?" She looked me over closely, "Have you eaten anything today?"

"I just got up."

She wiped the counter.

"What are you making?" I asked.

"Chili. But it won't be right until tomorrow. I ran out of chili powder. It's better the next day anyway. Do you want breakfast? I can make you some eggs?"

"Um, I don't know," I said, and just then I got an idea. "I, uh, I'm kind of in the mood for a veggie burger."

"Veggie—? Nonsense. If you want a burger I've got some good ground chuck."

"I've been eating too much red meat. I want a veggie burger. Do you think we could go to The Co-op?"

"In Bellflower? That's more than twenty-minutes each way."

"So it'll be five o'clock when I eat. Big deal."

"What about Benson's? It's closer. I'm sure they have veggie burgers."

"I want a selection."

"A selection?"

I nodded enthusiastically. Honestly, I was starving and the last thing I wanted to eat was a veggie burger, but I needed to get to The Co-op and the only way to get there was to have Nana Cole drive me.

Staring at me, I could tell she was making calculations. She'd promised to take care of me. This certainly qualified. I could also see her writing my interest in a 'selection' of veggie burgers off to a California thing. Although, I'd have to say that given the fact of The Co-op and yurts and women who saw auras, the area was being invaded by stereotypically Californian ideas.

"You're up to something."

"I am not."

She turned off the burner. "All right. Get ready," she said tersely.

"Thank you. Thank you."

"Just get ready."

Quietly, I struggled to get my jacket on. Nana Cole, who'd already gotten her purse and put her full-length puffer on, helped me into it. I stepped into the one boot I was going to wear. She wrapped a long scarf around my neck and a few minutes later—well, maybe it was a bit longer—we were in the Escalade. Reilly was still out in the yard somewhere. I figured he'd be fine for the hour we were gone. Mostly, I was thinking about how to reach into my pocket and get a pill and then how I could take it without being noticed.

"They're saying snow this weekend," Nana Cole said as we drove down the driveway past the orchard.

"You're kidding. It's spring. It was fifty degrees last week, wasn't it?" Well, at least forty-five.

"We've had snow as late as May." Then she asked, "Do you miss California?"

"Yes," I said, deciding not to be too obvious about how much I didn't want to be in Masons Bay. I mean, at a certain point it's just rude.

"You don't have a regular doctor. You need someone don't you?"

"Is there a clinic or something?" I needed to avoid medical professionals who sent bills.

"I'll get you in to see Dr. Blinski," she said.

"Isn't there a free clinic around here?"

"You're not destitute."

"Actually, I am."

"You'll go to see Dr. Blinski. My treat." Then she turned on the radio and we listened to Dr. Laura answer questions from her listeners. They'd call in and ask stupid questions—seriously, I think she had a producer ranking them by dumbness, practically brainless scoring the highest—and then Dr. Laura would scold them in a way that they seemed to enjoy. Normally, I would have begged to change the station—anything else, country, easy-listening—but I was just happy we were one our way.

By the time we got to The Co-Op, I was in a lot of pain. Seriously, it was torture level and I was ready to tell my captors where the microfilm was. My ankle was throbbing, my face hurt, and I ached all over like I'd been hit by a truck, which I kind of had been. Awkwardly, I got out of the SUV, turn sideways in the seat, put crutches out first, then good foot, then using a crutch to balance hopped out completely. I fell against the open door but stayed standing. A victory.

Nana Cole was already across the small parking lot and had gotten a cart. I started across the lot, by then she was in the store. I stopped, crutches tucked under my arms, I reached into the puffer jacket and felt around until I found a loose Perc. I popped it into my mouth and chewed it up.

I sighed with relief. The pain would be better in a few minutes. I wouldn't have to blab about the microfilm after all.

As I walked into The Co-op, the first thing I scoped out were the checkout lanes. One of the cashiers fit the description Sandy Edelson had given me: medium height, a little heavy. I could see that she was in her late thirties, had a large, pretty smile and eyes that were very light and smoky. I crutched over as closely I could. It looked like her name tag might say Audrey. It was hard to tell since she was checking someone out which meant she kept moving. I was pretty sure it was her, though.

As I struggled to catch up with Nana Cole, I tried to think about how to approach Audrey. Take her off guard or try to become her friend—well, there wouldn't be time for that. We'd be checking out. I'd have a couple minutes at best. So, I'd have to go with taking her off guard.

I caught up to Nana Cole in bulk goods. She was buying rice. She glanced up at me. "This is actually a good price."

"Uh-huh."

"I really don't understand this organic thing though," she said. "Food's food and cancer's cancer. One doesn't necessarily lead to the other."

I knew there were lots of reasons to eat healthy, avoiding cancer was only one of them. But my grandfather had died of colon cancer and I'd heard what you ate could be a reason for that. Nana Cole had fed him for nearly fifty years. It sounded like she was blaming herself or rather trying not to. Before I thought about it, I said, "Grandpa's cancer wasn't your fault Nana."

"I wasn't talking about that. I was talking about organic food. Why'd you have to bring up your grandfather?"

"I just, um, I don't know."

"Of course, it's not my fault he had cancer. Why would you think it was my fault?"

"I didn't—I thought you—can we just get the veggie burgers and leave?"

"We need to get some of those good potato chips. We're out all ready. And we might as well get those cookies you like. We're half way through the ones you bought the other day."

Since I'd been kind of busy getting run off the road and spending an eternity at the hospital, I suspected she was the one who'd eaten my snacks.

By the time we were at checkout, Nana Cole had filled half the cart and the Perc had kicked in, so I was feeling much, much less pain. There were two cashiers open. Unfortunately, the other cashier, the one who wasn't Audrey, had the shorter line.

"No, let's get in this line," I said, pointing to the longer line.

Nana Cole looked at me like I was crazy. "No, we'll get out faster this way."

"Trust me, this cashier is super fast."

She glared at me for a moment and then we got into Audrey's line. Of course, it took much longer for it to be our turn, which earned me some sideways looks from my grandmother. Finally, we were next.

Audrey looked up from her register and saw me. Even though she didn't know me, she asked, "What happened to you?"

I guess that wasn't weird since I was on crutches and there were tiny white Tampons shoved up my nose. Not to mention my eyes were purple on the way to black.

"Car accident," I explained.

"Did you hit a deer? You're not a Michigander until you hit a deer." Was it that obvious I was a Fudgie?

"No, I didn't," I said, softly. "You're Audrey, aren't you?"

She reached up and pinched her name tag. "Sure am."

"I need to talk to you."

"If you need to know where something is, just ask away," she said, cheerfully. She began running our things over a scanner.

"I need to talk to you about Sammy Hart."

Audrey's face sagged. I could feel Nana Cole turn to glare at me.

"Why do you—never mind." She chewed her lip a second then said, "I have a break coming. I can talk to you out in the parking lot in a couple of minutes."

She finished scanning our groceries and silently put everything into three paper bags. Then she put them into our cart. As we walked out, loud enough that people could hear, Nana Cole said, "Do you believe they don't have plastic bags here? Just ridiculous."

Once we were outside in the parking lot, her tone shifted, and she asked, "What was that about? Why do you have to talk to that woman?"

"Maybe you should wait in the car."

"Are you trying to buy drugs?"

"I said I wanted to talk to her about Sammy Hart. I said that right in front of you."

"You could still be buying drugs."

"From a woman in a health food store?"

"They're all hippies."

"Put the groceries in the car."

She narrowed her eyes at me.

"Please?"

With a sniff, she went ahead and did that while I wobbled on my crutches a few feet from the door. Audrey came out a minute or so later wearing a big winter parka and taking a long cigarette out of a pack. When she got to me she lit the cigarette, saying, "I was quit, for six years. Now I'm back at it worse than ever."

"You were seen having an argument with Sammy Hart. Outside a yoga studio."

"A lot of people look like me. You've made a mistake."

"Then why are you talking to me? I mentioned Sammy Hart and you agreed to come out here and talk to me."

Her mouth became an angry line. I could almost see her trying on a couple of other lies and then not liking them. "Okay. Yeah, that happened. Big deal."

"What were the two of you arguing about?"

Nana Cole had finished putting the groceries into the back of the Escalade and was now standing next to me. Audrey looked her over uncomfortably as she smoked.

"It's none of your business what I was fighting about with Sammy. Who are you anyway?"

"I work for The Conservancy. I found Sammy's body."

She looked at the trees and didn't say anything. "Okay. Yes, I had an argument with Sammy. I shouldn't have, I know that now."

"What was the argument about?"

"Nothing. I was being stupid."

"Is that what you told Detective Lehmann? That you were stupid?"

Audrey rolled her eyes and said, "Oh my God."

"Henry," Nana Cole said. Her tone told me she thought I was being too harsh.

Audrey looked at me now, her lip quivering. She'd smoked her cigarette down to the filter. "No one from the sheriff's office has talked to me about Sammy."

"No one—? But I told Detective—"

"You told him—? Oh God, I can't do this."

"You can't do what, Audrey?"

"This is such a mess."

"Where were you on February nineteenth? The day Sammy died?"

"Wait. You don't think—of course you do. You think I murdered Sammy. Oh, my lord."

"It was a Wednesday. Is that your regular day?"

"Usually."

"You didn't work that Wednesday?"

"No, I took the day off. I didn't want anyone to know."

"Duh, of course you didn't want anyone to know you were going to ki—"

"No, no, no... I went to see a lawyer. A *divorce* lawyer."

Then it began to fall into place for me. It was all so obvious. Sammy had to be involved with her husband. What I'd seen on Craigslist, on AOL, the whole 'must be discreet' thing. That was real. Common even. Bi-guys, gay guys, whatever they were, they all cheated on their wives. Audrey had been cheated on.

"You can prove that?" I asked. She had an alibi. Was it for the whole day?

"The lawyer is in Grand Rapids. I didn't want anyone around here to find out."

"They will eventually."

"Yes, I know but... you see, I changed my mind. Maybe I knew I would all along. Maybe that's why I went out of town. My husband, Chris, I've always known he had, uh, feelings that way. And, I knew sometimes he did things about them. I tried not to think about it, but I knew. The thing with Sammy. It was different. It seemed—I thought Sammy was going to take my husband away from me."

Nana said, "What? No, that can't—"

I interrupted her and asked Audrey point blank, "Did you have something to do with his death?"

I mean, seriously, she might have paid someone and gone to Grand Rapids so she'd have—

"No, oh my God, no. This is all so awful." She'd put out her cigarette long ago. Now she said, "I have to go back inside. They only give me five minutes for a break."

And with that she walked away. My grandmother looked at me, giving me classic stink eye. "You didn't want a veggie burger, you wanted to talk to that girl."

"Maybe," I admitted.

"Well, guess what you're having for dinner."

Chapter 19

"WHAT EXACTLY IS it you're up to?" Nana Cole asked after she'd plunked the naked veggie burger down in front of me.

"What do you mean?" I said, playing dumb. I was surprisingly good at playing dumb. Well, I surprised myself, maybe other people expected it.

"You know what I mean. You didn't just humiliate that poor woman for no good reason."

"I don't know that *I* humiliated her."

"She didn't want to be talking about those things, and you pushed her until she did."

"Yes, but she might have known something—"

"She didn't, though did she?"

Nana Cole was right. Audrey hadn't really known anything. Still, it had been valuable to talk to her.

"Don't you think it's suspicious that no one from the sheriff's office talked to her?"

"No, they probably don't know anything about—"

"*I* told Detective Lehmann. And he's done nothing about it. I think he should at least ex—"

"Oh no, you're not bringing that up with him."

"Why not?"

"It's not your business."

"But—"

"You don't know what people are like around here. It's not like the big city where you can just do whatever you want and nobody notices. People here have long memories. And the thing that poor woman said about her husband…" She shook her head. "That's what happens when people walk away from God."

I kept my mouth shut and ate my veggie burger. It was soggy but a lot more palatable than what she'd just said. Audrey's husband wasn't having sex with men because he didn't go to church. For all we knew, he was sitting in the first pew of some church every single Sunday. The assumption Nana Cole made really irked me.

Taking a deep breath, I decided not to think about that anymore. Nana Cole had given me a lot of the really good potato chips. That was something to focus on and be thankful for. I stuffed half of what was left into my mouth.

Yes, I should probably tell my grandmother about the reward, then my behavior would make more sense. But there was also a fifty-fifty chance knowing would just make things worse and she'd lock me in my room leaving me stuck staring at a young David Cassidy the rest of my life.

The pain was getting bad again, so after dinner I went upstairs and took a Percocet. Then another. Then I called Vinnie.

"Oh hi," he said when he picked up. "Listen I can't talk long. I'm going to happy hour at Marix. I've decided I want to bag myself a studio executive. They make a lot of money, don't they?"

"Someone tried to kill me last night."

"Oh my God, I *cannot* believe it! You won't let the conversation be about me for even two seconds."

"Um, sorry? I, uh, don't know how much studio executives make."

"Forget it, the moment has passed. *Who* tried to kill you?"

"I don't know. They forced me off the road and I almost ripped through a gas pump but hit a Pontiac Fiero instead."

"All right, let's recap. In our last conversation you found your cousin's dead body on another cousin's property, then you slept with your cousin, so my guess is your cousin tried to kill you."

"I didn't sleep with my cousin," I said, though to be honest I'd never checked Bill Touhy's family tree. "You're not taking this very seriously."

"I am, trust me. It's just that I'm also deciding what to wear to Marix's. Something that will attract rich creative types."

"Just wear something slutty."

"That doesn't help. You just described my entire wardrobe."

"Or better yet, just wear a clean white T-shirt and jeans."

"Really?"

"Oh yeah. If you're going to be a gold digger, you have to look like you couldn't care less about money. Nothing flashy, no designer labels. You need to look good, but not like you spent money on it or gave it any thought. White T, blue jeans. Cowboy boots if you have them."

"Darling, you're a lifesaver. Really. I have to go. I only have an hour."

"But, I—"

I stopped. I had a terrible realization. I'd become the annoying friend whose life swings from one disaster to another. Vinnie and I made fun of a people like that and then ran from them whenever we saw them in a bar. I was officially someone I would run from. How did that happen?

"You know what, Vinnie. Have a really good time."

"Thank you, dear. I will."

And with that, we hung up.

———

THE NEXT MORNING, I dreamed that my mother had stolen my bed and refused to give it back. I had no idea why she did that to me, but it was particularly cruel since I was in terrible pain and all I wanted to do was lie back down. Where was I going to sleep? How was I going to stop the pain?

I woke with a start and sat up. Yeah, there I was in my mother's teenaged bedroom. No one had stolen the bed. Reilly sat on his haunches giving me a look that said, "Do you really want to do this? The bed is still warm and cozy. All you have to do is lie back down."

He was a very persuasive dog, but I got up anyway. I hopped around the room on my one good foot until I found my cell in the front pocket of my jeans. It was around nine—which I thought was a much more reasonable hour than the day before —so I called Opal.

"I need a favor," I said when she picked up.

"I'm going to stop answering your calls."

"Seriously?"

"You still sound like you have a cold."

"My nose is still packed with cotton. Come on, do you want to find out who killed Sammy, or not?"

"Of course, I do."

"Then I need you to take me somewhere."

"Where?"

"I don't know."

"Is that north of 'who knows where' or west of 'dude, I'm lost'?"

"Where would you go to buy fire irons?"

"Amazon."

"And if you didn't want to wait two weeks for them to arrive? And you lived at Sammy's house in Bellflower."

"Keswick's, I guess. That's closest."

"What is that?"

"It's a big box hardware store like Home Depot."

"You don't have Home Depot?"

"No, we have Home Depot too. Do you want to drive fifty-five minutes?"

"Actually, you would be driving."

"Whatever."

"No, I want to try the closest one first."

"First? I'm not a chauffeur."

"Pick me up in half an hour."

At exactly nine thirty, there was a honk in the driveway. Reilly sat up and barked. I'd taken the last of the Percs—I wasn't doing at all well with my plan to not take pills for pain—and already had my coat on and was waiting by the door. I'd been planning to leave Reilly inside, but he bolted out the door when I opened it. The sky was cloudy, but it was above freezing so I decided not to worry about Reilly and I promised myself I wouldn't be gone long.

Opal's car sat in the driveway. It was one of those retro Volkswagen Beetles, red with black spots and plastic eyelashes attached to the headlights. It was meant to look like a ladybug.

"Your car is ridiculous," I said after I'd struggled into it.

"You look like an extra in a bad zombie movie."

"Let's just go."

"No."

"No? Why did you come then?"

"Why are we going to Keswick's?"

"To look at fire irons. I said that."

"Why are we looking at fire irons?"

"Because Sammy was killed with a fireplace poker. And then that poker showed up in Bev's car. But, at his house there's a brand-new set of fire irons with nothing missing. Someone replaced it. I want to try and find out who."

"What will that tell you?"

"I don't know. But I think it's important, don't you?"

She looked at me for a moment like she might throw me out of the ladybug, but then she started the engine. She turned the car around and we drove down the long, dirt driveway.

Next to the steering wheel, on the dashboard, was a plastic vase—one of the New Beetle's famous features. Opal's vase was filled with a red plastic rose.

"I'm guessing the ladybug has name?"

"Lydia."

"Lydia the ladybug. That's special."

"Shut it."

And then we were on our way to Bellflower. You would think we'd have spent the time talking about our families, what school was like for each of us, and the differences between California and Northern Lower Michigan—you know, basic getting to know you kind of stuff. But I had the distinct feeling Opal didn't want to get to know me, and she really wasn't my type of person anyway, so we were quiet a lot of the way.

Actually, I spent most of the ride trying to find a CD to play. Opal's taste in music varied wildly from '80s punk to rap to lesbian folk. None of which I wanted to listen to. Finally, I decided on the cast album for *Jesus Christ Superstar*—I'd passed it over three times in hopes of finding something better and finally gave up.

"Are you religious?" she asked when she recognized the music.

"God, no," I said.

"Okay, I just wondered. I mean you were at the pancake supper and, you know, this is the album you chose."

"I really don't think this drove a lot of people to church," I said, though honestly, I had no idea. It was *so* before my time.

"You never know what drives people to church."

"Oh my God, you're religious, aren't you?"

"There's nothing wrong with—"

"But you don't go to my grandmother's church. She told me that."

"I don't belong to any church, but I *am* a Christian."

"How?" I asked. "I'm sorry, I mean—no, I actually do mean how. How?"

"How can I be a Christian when I'm bisexual? Is that what you're trying to ask me?"

"Yeah, that."

"The Bible doesn't say very much about women having sex with women. It's really much more concerned with what you boys do with your wee-wees."

I glanced over at her suspiciously. This was not the way most Christians talked about sex. I also had no idea if she was right or wrong. Most of my biblical knowledge was second or thirdhand.

"Why were you at the pancake supper if you don't go to that church?"

"I thought it might be a good place to meet people."

"You were sitting alone."

"I didn't say I was *good* at meeting people."

"You know, if you were a little nicer I'm sure lots of people would want to meet you. Or at least some."

"Just shut up."

And then we were pulling into Keswick's gigantic parking lot. Seriously, pretty much everyone in Masons Bay could drive over and there'd still be room for other shoppers. I suppose it was important for these big places to have enormous parking lots whether they needed them or not. I mean, a football field-sized building with a tiny parking lot would look silly.

Opal parked like a million miles away. I glared at her, "Can't you find a closer space? In case you haven't noticed, I'm on crutches."

She rolled her eyes, turned the car back on and then drove up to the entrance. "Get out," she said when she stopped the ladybug.

"I'll wait for you."

"Whatever."

I struggled out of the car, crutches first, and then waited in front of the store. It was cold enough that I wished I'd worn a hat. But I hated wearing hats. They messed up my hair. But then I didn't much care for frozen ears either.

I watched Opal walk across the lot. She really was a weird girl. She was wearing an old army coat that she must have gotten from Goodwill; Doc Martens, which I think were in style when I was in grade school; and a granny dress. I mean, nothing she had on was even remotely in style. If this were L.A. I'd be completely humiliated being seen with her.

We walked through the automatic doors and I said, "Okay, so do you know where the fire irons are?"

"Well, when I rehabbed my house and put in the marble and gold fireplace—I don't know, they're probably over that way somewhere."

Glumly, we walked in the direction she'd pointed. It took a while, but we found the fire irons near a display of wood stoves and fireplaces you could install in your home. They had four different sets of fire irons. The cheapest was the exact kind I'd seen in Sammy's house—brass and black iron.

"These are the ones in Sammy's house," I said, pointing to the set.

She stood there a moment, and then said, "No, he had this set." She pointed to the most expensive one.

I reached over and picked out the poker. "Yeah, this is just like the one they found in Bev's car. This is just like the murder weapon."

"So, someone replaced the set."

"That's what it looks like."

"Can I help you with something?" I turned around and there was a teenage boy so clean cut he probably squeaked.

"Fabulous," I said, leaning on my crutches. "I was afraid we'd have to wander all of the store looking for help."

He cringed a little when I said 'fabulous.' I must have scared him.

"Oh, well, we pride ourselves on service here at Keswick's."

"Wonderful." Another cringe. "I need to know who bought one of these fire iron sets on February nineteenth or twentieth."

"What?"

It was a straight-forward question, so I tried rephrasing, "Someone bought this set either February nineteenth or twentieth. I need to find out who that was."

"No. I can't give you that information."

"Sweetheart." That brought the biggest cringe yet. I was enjoying this a little. "You just said you pride yourselves on service."

"If you'd like to buy the set—"

"No, neither of us have a fireplace. I want to know who bought a set on February—"

"Yes, I know what you're asking. I can't tell you that. Our customers' privacy is also important at Keswick's."

"Oh my God," Opal sighed heavily. "I can't believe I'm doing this. Is Cheryl Ann working today?"

Squeaky Clean glowered at her. "Yes. I guess you want me to get her."

"If you wouldn't mind."

He walked off stiff with anger.

Opal said to me, "You owe me for this."

"I'm not splitting the reward."

"Don't worry. I'm one of the people offering it, that means I can't claim it. Okay?"

"Sure." But I still didn't like the idea of owing her. When you owed people things they had a habit of collecting at exactly the wrong time. "This is a weird store."

"What you mean?"

"I mean, it's like a hardware store, but they have lots of things that aren't hardware. Like women's clothes—did you notice that? Maybe on the way out we could take a look—"

"No. Just no. I don't need a gay best friend to dress me."

"Well you need *someone* to dress you. You're a disaster."

"Opal! I can't believe you're here," Cheryl Ann nearly squealed as she hurried over. "You look great by the way."

What planet was she on? It's like neither of them had ever seen a single episode of *What Not to Wear*.

"Thank you," Opal said. I noticed that she didn't return the compliment, though Cheryl Ann was dressed in a green uniform and wore a tag that said ASSISTANT MANAGER. Which, given the circumstances, meant she looked as good as she could.

"There's something we're trying to find out," Opal said, trying to smile as she said it. Seriously, she needed flirting lessons in addition to a new wardrobe. "Someone took the fire iron set out of Sammy's house the day he was killed and replaced it with this set here. We want to know who purchased this set on February nineteenth or twentieth."

Seriously? She just gave everything away. Now Cheryl Ann could just say no, go look up the information and turn it in to the sheriff and get the reward herself. I wanted to slaughter Opal right there in the aisle at Keswick's.

"Well, I'm not supposed to—"

"Opal would be so grateful," I said.

"You would?" she said to Opal as though I wasn't even standing there.

"Yes, I would be grateful." Again with the pathetic smile.

"Well, um, if they paid cash there's not much I can do. But if they used a credit card, I could find out."

"Would you look?" I asked, giving Cheryl Ann what she should have been getting from Opal. Look at me, leading by example.

"I'll be right back," Cheryl Ann said, scurrying off.

When she was out of earshot, Opal said, "This may come as a surprise to you, but being bisexual doesn't mean I want to sleep with everyone I meet."

"She's sweet. You should give her a chance." She was also not attractive or intelligent, but given where we were I thought sweet was hitting the jackpot.

"Mind your own business, okay?"

I rolled my eyes at her and said, "God this place is depressing."

"It's a big box store. You're not supposed to want to move in."

"I don't mean Keswick's—although you're right, it *also* is depressing. I meant, this whole place is depressing, Masons Bay, Bellflower, Wyandot County. Ugh."

"Then leave."

"I'm trying to."

"How did you end up here anyway?"

"The whole thing was stupid. I took one too many Oxys and my roommate thought I was ODing so he called the paramedics, which landed me at USC hospital and my mother showed up and convinced them to 5150 me—trust me I was *not* trying to kill myself. That's how she forced me to come here. She's got the stupid idea in her head that this is somehow saving my life."

"How old are you?"

"Twenty-four."

"Yeah. No one *forced* you to do anything. You're an adult.

172

You may not like the choices you had to make, but you're here because you chose to be."

God, she was such a bitch, which was a little confusing because I usually really liked bitchy girls. Of course, they didn't usually direct their bitchiness at me.

There was a display of lawn furniture a ways down, so I tottered over and sat down.

Not having anything else to do, Opal followed me. "So you're a drug addict?" she asked when she sat down.

"No. I'm not."

"You've overdosed, and you called me for the number for a drug dealer. You're checking off the boxes."

I carefully put my bad foot up on the redwood coffee-table that was part of the display. "I'm just having fun, okay?"

"Yeah, you look like you're having a blast."

Cheryl Ann hurried over to us. Her face was pale, and she looked like she might puke. "Okay, um, you *cannot* tell anyone this. I mean, I could lose my job."

"Okay. Promise," I said. I doubted I'd keep the promise long, but it was worth making.

"Rudy Lehmann."

"What? Detective Rudy Lehmann?"

"Well, yeah. I don't think there's another Rudy Lehmann in the county."

Chapter 20

WHEN WE WALKED into the sheriff's office things looked way different. There were three new people sitting at the half-dozen desks outside the offices. A huge increase over the last time I was there. I hobbled up to Detective Lehmann's office with Opal in tow. He was sitting at his desk reading the *Wyandot Eagle*.

I cleared my throat. He looked up and glanced at each of us, fully taking in my rather pathetic state.

"You're here for your statement? You know, you really could have waited a few days. There's no rush."

"I'd like to make an application for the reward."

"Really? You think you have information that will lead to an arrest?"

"Yes."

"All right, what is it?"

"You did it."

"Oh my God," Opal said. "I can't believe you said that. You don't *know* he did it. You don't *know*—"

"Shut up," I whispered at her.

"I guess that's a joke. It's not very funny," Lehmann said.

"I'm not joking. You had access to the crime scene and you bought a set of fire irons on February nineteenth, replacing the one with the missing poker. The poker that killed Sammy Hart. There's only one reason you'd—"

Lehmann hesitated a moment and then went over and closed the door. "You don't know what you're talking about. You shouldn't even be involved in this."

"Why did you kill him?"

"I didn't. You're wrong about this. All of it."

"See, I told you," Opal said.

"Why did you replace the fire irons then? Huh? Explain that—"

"Henry, let him talk."

I ignored her. "Were you involved with Sammy?" I dramatically put air quotes around *involved*. I mean, it seemed a reasonable question. Everyone else in the county was doing the dead man.

Lehmann though looked at me as though he didn't understand what I was saying. "No, I wasn't *involved* with Sammy Hart." He said, returning my air quotes.

Shaking his head, he said, "Look, Audrey called me about the conversation she had with—"

"Audrey? Audrey who works at The Co-op?"

"Yes. Audrey Caine is my sister."

"Oh."

"The thing is… She'd come to me a week or so before Sammy disappeared. She told me about the affair he and Chris were having. She was upset, very upset, a couple of times she said she wanted to kill Sammy."

"So, you killed him for her?"

"Don't be an idiot," Lehmann said.

"I'm not an idiot."

"You kind of are," Opal said.

"Shut up."

"When Sammy was reported missing," Detective Lehmann began, ignoring our bickering. "I thought Audrey might have… done something. So I made sure to be the one to go into his house. Just as I'd feared, there was evidence that Sammy had been murdered. Blood. The missing poker. I was sure it was Audrey so I cleaned up the scene. I shouldn't have, I know it was wrong. I just—she's my sister."

"But she was in Grand Rapids," Opal said, beating me to the punch.

"What?"

"She was in Grand Rapids talking to a divorce lawyer," I said.

"So she couldn't have done it?"

I stared at him, "Don't the two of you ever talk?"

"I wasn't going to *ask* if she killed him. If I knew for a fact she killed him I would be legally bound to arrest her."

"That's where you draw the line?" I said. "You concealed evidence, you destroyed evidence, that's all illegal too. Isn't it?"

"Let's not dwell on that," Opal said. "So now that you know your sister didn't kill Sammy, do you think you can investigate his death properly?"

"Of course, yes," he said.

Oh great, I thought, *more competition.* Opal was not helpful at all. Trying to turn this back to my advantage, I asked, "Did you learn anything from the crime scene? You know, before you destroyed it?"

"I can't really divulge—"

"Oh, I think you can," I said.

Realizing the position he was now in, he sat back and sighed heavily. I almost felt sorry for him. I doubted he had much experience with murder investigations and to think that one of the very few murder cases he'd ever work was a crime he thought was committed by his own—

"Um, well, from the way things looked Sammy was walking from the parlor toward the foyer when he was struck from behind."

"How many times?"

"Once. We know that from the autopsy," he said. "I think he was probably leading the murderer to the door. So they might have argued—"

"Why do you think they argued?"

He shrugged a shoulder. "It's kind of common before bashing someone over the head."

"Good point."

"Anyway, I think Sammy was trying to get rid of this person, and whoever it was grabbed the poker and hit Sammy over the head with it."

"So you don't think it was planned?"

"It doesn't appear that way."

"And then how did they get Sammy out of the house?"

"The body was dragged through the kitchen to the garage. I think they put down the back seat in the Land Rover and laid down garbage bags before they put the body in. They drove it out to the Sheck farm and dumped the body. Then they returned to the house and put the Rover back in the garage."

Something bothered me about that, but it didn't register right then. Instead, I asked, "There's not a lot of evidence in the car?"

"We haven't actually—"

"I see."

"And they made no attempt to clean up?"

"No, they did. They just did a terrible job and I think they may have left in a hurry."

"Do you think it was one person or two?"

"I'm not sure."

"Well, how did you think your sister managed?"

"I assumed she called Chris and got him to help."

That stopped me. He really thought his sister could call her husband and say some version of, "Hi hon, just killed your boyfriend. Come help me clean up," and he'd have shown up. Weird.

"Did you talk to the neighbors?" Opal asked.

"Yeah, why didn't anyone see anything?" I joined in.

"The neighbors either weren't home or they're snowbirds. There wasn't a lot to see, anyway. The garage is connected to the house."

I knew that. I'd been there. I should have—

"Well, thank you for being honest with us," Opal said.

"Can I have a copy of your file?"

"No, that's not possible."

"Seriously? I could tell the sheriff what you did."

His jaw got tight. I thought he might break a tooth.

"I'll stay late and copy it. You can pick it up tomorrow."

———

"I CAN'T BELIEVE you just blackmailed a sheriff's deputy. That's just not smart," Opal said as we drove back to Masons Bay.

"What do you mean, not smart? I'm going to have his complete file tomorrow. Including the autopsy."

"And what if he's the killer? Did you think of that?"

Actually, I hadn't.

"Why would he—" I stopped. It was obvious why he'd have killed Sammy Hart. He loved his sister and Sammy was ruining her marriage.

"All we really know is that he cleaned up the crime scene, which he could have done right after he killed Sammy," Opal said, advancing her theory.

I was feeling sick to my stomach. "Could we go to a drugstore? I have a prescription I need to fill."

She gave me the side-eye.

"It's from a doctor."

"All prescriptions are from doctors. Doesn't mean they're good for you."

We needed to get off *that* subject. "Do you really think Detective Lehmann is Sammy's killer?"

"No. Not a chance."

"Then why did you just—"

"He seemed genuinely surprised that his sister had an alibi. And happy she wasn't a killer."

That was actually true.

Then we were on the main drag in Masons Bay and Opal pulled the ladybug into a small parking lot. There were several businesses in an older, cream-colored, clapboard building: an electrical shop, a bike repair, a real estate office and Penny-wise Drugs—which to me sounded like a bargain basement dealer.

We went into the pharmacy, which was small and didn't look

at all penny wise. I gave the pharmacist my prescription and was told it would be about five minutes. I didn't see how that was possible, in L.A. it always took forty-five. But then, everything in L.A. took forty-five minutes. It was just a fact of life.

Opal was looking at a spinning rack of romance novels—on closer inspection Christian romance novels—and I was trying to get in her face, so I could make gagging noises when my phone rang. I glanced at the tiny screen and saw that it was Nana Cole. Since she never called me, I decided it might be a good idea to pick up. Someone could be dead.

"Hello."

"Henry? Henry is that you?"

"Yes, of course it's me. You called me."

"Where are you? You snuck out."

"I did not sneak out. You were off gardening or something." Really, I hadn't given her a second thought.

"You have to come back. I got you a doctor's appointment, like I told you I would. We have to be there at two o'clock. And you need to have lunch first."

I thought about turning the doctor visit down and making an effort to find a clinic, but Nana Cole had said she'd treat and, honestly, I really, really, really wanted to get the packing out of my nose.

"All right, I'll be home in time."

I flipped the phone closed and stared at Opal. She was reading the first few pages of a book called *The Cherished Heart*. Abruptly she said, "I think the husband did it," which made me wonder if the book she was holding was actually a mystery.

"Which husband?"

"Audrey's husband."

"Oh, of course. But why would he kill Sammy? They were involved."

"Are you really that naïve? People kill people they have sex with all the time. I mean, maybe Sammy was dumping Audrey's husband for Richard?"

"Or Phil."

She looked up from the book. "What? No! Really?"

"Yes, really," I said, somewhat pleased I'd known something she hadn't. "He told me they'd been together for a year."

"Well that explains a lot. I mean, Sammy and Phil were together a lot. I just—"

"Do they each know about the other? Phil and Richard? And Chris for that matter."

"I don't know."

My name got called and I went up to the counter and picked up my Oxy. The prescription cost twelve dollars and I was able to sneak it onto my last credit card. When we got outside, I asked, "What time is it?"

"Almost noon."

"I have a doctor's appointment. You better drop me at my grandmother's."

"Are you kidding? We're going to the bookstore to see Phil first."

"But—"

"I'm not a taxi service." And then, almost contradicting herself, she said, "Don't worry, you'll get where you're going with plenty of time to spare."

The bookstore was a whole two blocks away, so she was probably right. We'd be fine. Absurdly, we got in the car, drove the two blocks, parked, and got out. When we walked into the darling little bookstore, Phil *and* Richard were standing at the front counter.

"Oh, my Lord, what happened to you?" Richard asked when he got a good look at me.

"He *claims* someone deliberately ran him off the road," Opal said, oozing cynicism. I wanted to slap her.

"Thank you. That's what happened," I said, not looking at Richard. I didn't want to acknowledge him after seeing him at Ronnie Sheck's. "I'm getting close. I think I've scared Sammy's killer."

"Who do you think it is?" Richard asked.

I didn't want to give too much away, not right off the bat.

"It might have something to do with Sammy's being beaten-up in 1999."

"But we all know about that," Richard said. "It's hardly a secret."

"It was terrible. A friend being the victim of a hate crime," Phil said. "And before you say anything, they happen *every*where. Even in places like L.A."

"It wasn't a hate crime," I said. "I mean, it wasn't nice but… Rupert Beckett beat him up. He admitted it to me."

"Did he really?"

"Why?"

"Why did he admit it? Because the statute of limitations is up. He said statue but—"

"Why did he beat Sammy up?"

"I think it was a family thing. Something to do with the land on Swan Lake."

"There is no Swan Lake. That's a ballet," Opal pointed out. Know-it-all.

"Duck?"

"Goose. You mean, Goose Lake."

"Okay, that."

"Well, that land is going to The Conservancy. There's nothing the Becketts can do about it now," Phil said.

Which reminded me that Phil got everything, the house, the furnishings, the car—suddenly, something that had been nagging at me came into focus.

"The Land Rover."

"What about it?" Phil asked.

"You said you don't drive it."

"I don't. It just feels wrong."

"You haven't driven it at all since Sammy disappeared?"

"No."

"It's been sitting in the driveway the whole time?"

"Yes."

"Detective Lehmann said it was in the garage the day Sammy disappeared. So, who moved it?"

Chapter 21

"YOUR MOTHER CALLED," Nana Cole said, flipping through a *People* magazine. "She's very upset about your accident."

"It wasn't an accident. Someone tried to kill me."

We were sitting in Dr. Blinski's waiting room. His office was at the front of an old house made of the same kind of round stones as Nana's porch and smelled like mothballs.

"You're very dramatic. Just like her."

"Are you trying to make me angry?" I asked, I had made it clear several times that I did not like being compared to my mother. More than several. A myriad. A myriad of myriads.

"The two of you are too much alike. That's why you don't get along."

"We're not at all alike." I said. My mother was a mess of a woman who'd had too many bad boyfriends and too many dead-end jobs. I was a student of life. Or at least, I would be when I figured out what that meant.

Honestly, I did not understand the relationship between my mother and grandmother. In my lifetime, they'd never gotten along. Nana Cole objected to almost every decision my mother made and said so. I remember the few visits we made being filled with screaming arguments, slamming doors and flying dinner plates.

I asked the obvious question. "Why are you suddenly

getting along with her? The two of you have never agreed on anything."

"It's easier to get along with people when you have a common goal. Your mother and I both love you."

I shifted in my seat. I wished she hadn't said that. Or said it in that way. I felt a little like the Wicked Witch of the West after a bath. But I wasn't ready for my heart to melt. I liked things the way they were. I liked hating them both. It was simple. It made sense. It was something of a family tradition.

Loving them was confusing and difficult and required forgiving their frequently annoying, frequently *bad* behavior.

A gray-haired nurse came out and called my name. I got up onto my crutches. Nana Cole stood up as though she was going in with me.

"Where do you think you're going?"

"I'm paying for this. I should be able to go in."

"No, I don't think so."

She gave me an icy glare but decided not to make a scene in front of the nurse. I turned and made my way through the door being held open for me. The nurse led me to the single exam room, which also seemed to serve as the doctor's office. Across from the exam table, sat a roll top desk pushed up against the wall. Seriously, I expected Andy Griffith to come in and tell me I was on some new reality show about a country doctor.

The nurse helped me up onto the table, took my crutches, and leaned them against the wall. Then she left, so I waited. And waited. Finally, there was a knock on the door and Dr. Blinski came in. He was a small man of nearly seventy with more hair in his nose and ears than on his head.

"I understand you had an accident?"

I didn't correct him, I was getting tired of correcting people and it didn't matter. I knew what happened.

"So, I can see that you've got a broken nose. Those are two impressive shiners."

"The packing is supposed to come out."

"Yes, all right. The splint stays on though. Don't take that off for a few more weeks."

"What splint?" I had no idea what he was talking about. My ankle was wrapped in a couple of ace bandages.

"Your nose. The tape on your nose is a splint."

"Oh, okay. How long do I have to leave it on?"

"Two weeks. Two and half would be better."

Damn, it was itchy and not remotely attractive. Though I hadn't thought a lot about it. Taking all the Percs had helped with that.

The doctor had been fishing around a tray on a table next to the door. When he turned around he had a pair of tweezers in one hand. Mouth open and glasses sliding down his nose, he gently pulled each of the cotton tubes out of my nose. Despite being what Vinnie referred to as "nearly-dead," Dr. Blinski was doing a good job. He managed not to cause me any more pain and I was now able to breathe.

"From the bruising it looks like you hit your face on the steering wheel. You were driving Emma's Ford truck?"

"I was."

"Hmmmm. Totaled?"

"She says not."

He shook his head, and then got an instrument out of a drawer and looked up each of my nostrils. He made appreciative noises as though he was happy with what he saw. Taking the instrument out of my nose, he said, "That's coming along nicely."

I felt like I should say thank you, but I couldn't figure out for what exactly.

"You were wearing a safety belt?"

"I was."

Without asking, he lifted up my shirt. "Oh yeah, you've got quite a bit of bruising. Still, it's better than the days when people didn't wear safety belts. The things I saw. People aren't meant to fly through windshields, let me tell you."

That seemed fairly obvious, but I smiled anyway.

Then he undid the ace bandages holding my ankle together. When he was done it was a terrible sight. Swollen and unsightly. Purple and blue, yellow and red. I hadn't been aware my body could turn that many different colors. Shit, I was a freaking rainbow flag.

"Are you keeping it elevated?"

"Yes, absolutely." That wasn't true exactly. I'd been doing a lot of running around most of which didn't include putting my leg in the air.

"I'm going to give you a boot," he said, and left the room. For a moment, I thought he meant he was throwing me out, which seemed very rude since I'd done little more than sit there. I hadn't been at all offensive.

A couple of minutes later he came back with a huge, gray boot. It had Velcro up and down the front and looked like something an extra would wear in *The Empire Strikes Back*.

"This should help you put weight on your ankle."

Quickly, he fit the boot on me. It felt kind of weird, but I was able to stand on the ankle, which meant I could say goodbye to the crutches and hello to walking like Frankenstein's monster.

"How does it feel?"

"It's okay. I mean it hurts but—" Always tell a doctor it hurts. You never know—

"Are you in a lot of pain?"

I nodded, trying to make it seem like I didn't want to say.

"What did they give you at the hospital? Nothing but Tylenol is my guess."

"It doesn't really work."

"No, it doesn't." Under his breath he said, "Fools." Then he sat down at his desk to write me a prescription for twenty 10s. Hallelujah!

I tried not to be visibly excited as I took the prescription. "Thank you. I think these will help."

"I know they will," he assured me. "Why don't you come see me in about three weeks. If you need a refill before then just give me a call."

If I need a refill? You bet your ass I would need a refill. I was positive I'd just found a more reliable dealer than Ronnie Sheck. Hallelujah!

A minute or so later, I was in the waiting room with Nana Cole. She walked over to the receptionist's window where the nurse took the money. The bill was well over two hundred dollars. That'll teach my grandmother to say 'my treat' when it comes to a doctor.

After that, we went home. I didn't dare ask to go anywhere, I didn't want her catching on about my trying to find Sammy's killer or the reward. I would have liked to try and find Chris Caine, Audrey's husband. It was entirely possibly he knew some- thing, maybe even something important. How was I going to find him though?

I mean, there was the phone book sitting in a short book- case in the living room, but I didn't want to show up at the guy's house when his wife was there. I could try to go to his job—but I didn't know where he worked. And that left… not a lot.

When we got home, I didn't even have to call Reilly, he just came running as soon as we reached the house. Life was already getting easier with the boot. I limped a little, but it wasn't too bad. Inside, I gave the dog a treat and we went upstairs. Well, I started to—

"You could say thank you, you know."

"For the ride?" I asked, though I knew what she meant.

"I paid for the doctor's visit."

"Yes, that's why I went. Because you promised to pay."

"And shouldn't you thank me for that?"

"I did what you wanted me to do to. Are you going to thank me for that?" I knew I was being an awful shit, but I couldn't resist.

"Dinner is at six," she said through gritted teeth.

"Thank you."

"For?"

"Telling me when dinner is. See you then."

Then I limped upstairs.

The thing about parents—or in this case grandparents—is that if you don't make their controlling your life as agonizing as humanly possible they'll just do it more and more. And that eventually leads to a long lecture about how it's time to grow up and start making your own decisions—ignoring the fact that they haven't let you do just that. The wisest course of action is terrorizing them to the point where they barely want to speak to you.

In my room, or rather my mother's room, I pulled out my iBook and hopped onto the bed. I'd had an idea about how I could find Chris Caine. I surfed my way over to craigslist.org and clicked on PERSONALS: MEN SEEKING MEN. I thought it very likely Chris Caine had an ad there and that I could find it.

There were certain things I knew that would help. I knew he was married and I knew that he was around his wife's age: late thirties. And, because Sammy was much older than that, I had an inkling Chris liked older men—a big ick in my book but to each his own. At least it would narrow things down quite a bit.

I scanned through the ads, many of which were oddly specific. I wondered how, in an area so small, men could ask for such specific quirks. But I guess if you didn't ask you never got. After reading through ten or twelve posts, I wondered if I should start introducing the posters to each other. Some of them definitely matched. Of course, they might already have made that match themselves, regretted it, and were here online to try again.

I found an ad that might be Chris Caine: **39, bi, looking for older, you host**. It was from a few weeks back. That made sense. It would be odd if he'd been trolling for sex around the time Sammy's body was found. I mean, he must have felt some remorse, right?

I had to create an account to respond.

Honestly, I'd never used Craigslist before. Why would I? All I had to do was get to West Hollywood, pop in and out of a couple of bars, never buy a drink, and take my pick of men to go home with. And that's not bragging; it's simple math. I was twenty-four. Twenty-four equals attention. I wasn't going to need to buy a drink in West Hollywood for at least another year. Maybe two if I could remember to moisturize and lie about my age.

And yes, the men who bought me drinks were much older than me, making me the tiniest bit like Chris Caine. But let's be frank. I almost never went home with any guy over thirty—very often I went home with someone who hadn't bought me any drinks at all. I call that integrity.

Anyway… Once I'd made up a login and agreed to some terms I didn't read, I was able to respond to the posting: Hey, I'm 55, gay and I live alone. If you want to get to know me my AIM screen name is LAMOOCH. After I answered, I dug back into the list. I found a couple other possibilities. But honestly, it was the first one that seemed most likely. I replied to the other two anyway.

Hopefully, it wouldn't take long to start getting responses. I snuck into my stash and took an Oxy. The pain was not as bad as it had been, but who knew how long I'd have to wait for this guy to—

Actually, it didn't take long at all. I was floating on a lovely cloud—humming along with some classic Madonna—when my computer mooed (the sound I'd chosen to indicate I had a message). I looked into the AIM chat box—it took a moment to focus—and saw that JAXOFF69 had messaged me:

JAXOFF69 (4:19:32 PM): Suck U off?

Ah, romance. This was why I preferred bars. "Can I buy you a drink?" usually preceded "Can I suck you off?" by quite a bit. Okay, stop that. I had to figure out if JAXOFF69 was Audrey's husband.

LAMOOCH (4:20:13 PM): Are you married?

JAXOFF69 (4:20:44 PM): No? U?"

I pondered for a bit. Did that mean he wasn't married? Or did that mean he was lying about being married?

LAMOOCH (4:21:15 PM): Not married. Can U host?

JAXOFF69 (4:21:25 PM): Yes. Come over.

Okay, well, this was definitely not the right person.

LAMOOCH: (4:21:33 PM): I like married men.

JAXOFF69 (4:22:05 PM): Like 3way?

God no, that's disgusting. I decided not to answer. I didn't think this was the guy I was looking for. I went ahead and closed the chat box. I lay back on the bed, pet Reilly on the head, and maybe took a little nappy.

A new moo woke me. I had a bad feeling it was going to be JAXOFF69 again. People on the Internet didn't always get it when you wanted them to go away. Another downside from a bar. In a bar you just wandered off and they watched. No one could put a positive spin on that and hope you'd just lost your Internet connection.

After I blinked my eyes a few dozen times, I looked at the AIM chat box.

BUILDER64 (5:24:46 PM): hi

LAMOOCH (5:25:13 PM): hi

BUILDER64 (5:25:55 PM): U like my ad?

I had no idea which ad had been his and I suppose asking would have been a bad idea. I went generic.

LAMOOCH (5:26:14 PM): You sound sexy

BUILDER64 (5:26:55 PM): U2. RU discrete?

That was wrong. I hopped over to my mother's old desk and snagged a yellowed paperback copy of Webster's leftover from her high school days. Yeah, yeah, there was a dictionary somewhere on my computer, but I just couldn't—anyway, I looked up discrete and yes, he was spelling it wrong. I really didn't think he was asking if I was a complete and separate entity onto myself.

LAMOOCH (5:28:47 PM): I'm discreet.

BUILDER64 is away at 5:30:12 PM.

Okay, I thought. Don't correct his spelling. It offends him. Then he was back.

BUILDER64 (5:32:10 PM): What do U like?

'People who don't ask that question' was my response if I got asked that in a bar. Negotiating sex was a big enough challenge in person. Doing it over fiber optic cable was nearly impossible.

LAMOOCH (5:32:50 PM): Do you have a wife?

BUILDER64 (5:33:15 PM): yes. sigh.

LAMOOCH (5:33:34 PM): Does she know you like guys?

BUILDER64 (5:34:14 PM): yes

My heart leapt a little. This might actually be Chris Caine. How could I be sure?

LAMOOCH (5:34:42 PM): And she's okay with this?

BUILDER64 (5:34:50 PM): Sort of. It's complicated.

It was complicated with Audrey, that was true. I decided to change directions for a moment.

LAMOOCH (5:35:20 PM): What do you build?

BUILDER64 (5:35:40 PM): Construction.

I assumed he meant he was a construction worker and built a lot of things. Well, that seemed like a field where he wouldn't be telling his co-workers much about his sex life.

How could I find out more? I couldn't ask his wife's name. That would be too obvious. I couldn't ask where she worked or whether she had a brown or possibly red car. I struggled to think whether there was any other detail that might give this away.

BUILDER64 (5:36:35 PM): Do U have gray hair?

Do I have gray hair? Why on earth would—oh that's right. I'd told him I was fifty-five. Well, of course, I had gray hair.

LAMOOCH (5:36:15 PM): Yes.

BUILDER64 (5:36:20 PM): Everywhere?

I had no idea if old guys got gray hair everywhere. And, honestly, I didn't want to know. But, since it seemed like he wanted it, I said yes to that. Then, I got a very simple idea and wondered why I didn't think of it before.

LAMOOCH (5:37:02 PM): My name is Richard.

BUILDER64 (5:36:40 PM): Richard the librarian in Bellflower?

Ah shit. I should have picked a different name. Wait though, if he knew Richard the librarian then he knew Sammy. And that made him the right person.

LAMOOCH (5:36:59 PM): No. I'm not from here.

BUILDER64 (5:37:20 PM): Snowbird?

LAMOOCH (5:38:05 PM): Sort of. What is your name?

BUILDER64 (5:39:33 PM): Chris.

There it was. It was him. Now, I had to decide if I should try to find out anything he knows on AIM or if I should try to meet him. Meet him. It would be harder for him to get away from me if he didn't want to talk to me.

LAMOOCH (5:40:10 PM): I want to meet you.

BUILDER64 (5:40:19 PM): I can cum over.

No, you can't.

LAMOOCH (5:40:45 PM): Coffee first. Drip.

BUILDER64 (5:41:02 PM): Really?

LAMOOCH (5:41:15 PM): Bad experiences.

BUILDER64: (5:42:09 PM): When?

We haggled back and forth until we agreed to meet at Drip the next afternoon at four. Now all I had to do was figure out how to get myself there.

Chapter 22

OPAL CALLED me the next morning at nine.

"Why are you calling me?" I asked, still half-asleep. I was all twisted up in sheets, blankets, a gigantic dog and pillows to elevate my ankle. I wouldn't have been able to get to the phone, except I'd fallen asleep at like two in the morning while leaving Vinnie a message.

"I have a life, you know," she said, although that didn't explain why she was calling.

"Okay."

"I figured at some point today you're going to call me and ask for a ride. I thought I'd find out when that might happen so I can plan my day."

"Well, I don't know yet. I mean, I need to be at Drip at four o'clock, but you can't be with me."

"I can't—You have a date?" she guessed. "You want me to drive you to a date?"

"It's not a date. I mean, he thinks it's a date, but it's not. It's with Audrey's husband, Chris Caine."

"You're going on a date with someone's husband?"

"I just said it's not a date. He was seeing Sammy before he was killed. He might have information."

"Why can't I be with you if it's not a date?"

193

"Because he *thinks* it's a date. I said that didn't I? Why are you making me repeat myself?"

"So, I'm just supposed to drop you off at Drip and then come back half an hour later?"

"Don't be stupid. You can sit at another table."

"I'm supposed to work at five. You'll only have about twenty minutes. Fifteen would be better."

"Where do you work?"

"I work at Pastiche in Masons Bay. We have to get from Bellflower to your grandmother's house with enough time for me to—"

"Isn't Pastiche a clothing boutique?"

"Yes."

Before I could stop myself, I said, "You have absolutely no fashion sense."

"Don't be one of those gays."

"One of what gays?"

"The ones who think because they got called a girl in gym class they know everything about women."

I wanted to point out that we weren't talking about women we were talking about clothes, but I really needed the ride. By way of apology I said, "Never mind."

"I'll pick you up at three-thirty. And dress appropriately, it's supposed to snow."

"Snow? But it's April."

"It's Michigan," she said, hardly an explanation, and then hung up.

I pushed myself into a sitting position and Reilly jumped off the bed. Watching me, he bounced around, tongue hanging out, excited to be going out. I was still groggy and slightly annoyed that dogs could go from dead asleep to cheerfully awake in a matter of seconds. I pulled a cardigan over my flannel pajamas—another of my grandfather's sweaters, one that I would never have worn in L.A. no matter how cold it got.

In my boot I clumped down the stairs and headed toward the kitchen to let Reilly out. When I got there, Bev was sitting with Nana Cole. Both looked tense and aggravated.

"What's happened?"

"Take your dog out and then come have a cup of coffee with us."

I did what I was told—with someone like Nana Cole it was good to occasionally do as she asked. It kept her on her toes. I watched Reilly hurry out to the thick old tree next to the pole garage and then pee on it—one of his favorite spots. Thankfully, he was fast in the mornings. Just wanted to relieve himself and then get back inside. It was too chilly for adventures or exercise.

We went back into the kitchen and I quickly fed Reilly, then sat down in front of the coffee Nana Cole had poured me.

"The Becketts are contesting Sammy's will," Bev said.

"Can they do that?" I asked, estate law not being one of my hobbies.

"It was Phil Robins who told me. He's the executor so he got the call from their attorney. Is that coffee cake on the counter?"

"It is," Nana Cole said. "Cherry cheese. Let me get you some." She stood up and went over to the counter. For a moment, she busied herself with plates and forks.

"Did Phil talk to his attorney?" I asked.

"Yes. The attorney questions whether they have standing. Normally, to contest a will you have to be a close relative, sibling or a child. But in this case, had Sammy not written a will the money would have gone to Rupert Beckett Sr., so he *could* have standing as Sammy's uncle."

Uncle? I thought we were all cousins. Someone really needed to draw me a family tree.

"Yes, but there's more to it than that," Nana Cole said, setting the coffee cake in the middle of the table. She'd cut pieces and put them on plates for each of us.

"This looks delicious, Emma," Bev said.

"Because Sammy left most of his estate to his 'friend,' there is a question as to whether there was undue influence."

"But they were... together," I said, my cheeks flushing. "They were more than friends. And it's what Sammy wanted."

"The court does not recognize that kind of relationship,"

Bev said. "In fact, it's illegal in Michigan to have a sex with someone of the same gender. An illegal relationship fits the definition of undue influence."

"Well, none of this should affect the land he left to The Conservancy," Nana Cole said. "That's not an immoral relationship."

I didn't like that she'd just shifted from legality to morality. They were vastly different things. But I didn't say anything, instead I took a bite of the coffee cake. It tasted wonderful but sat in my stomach like a rock.

"It's likely the entire will would be thrown out," Bev said. "Depending on the judge, of course. They're very conservative around here."

I glanced at Nana Cole. She usually loved conservative anything. But here her own views were denying—

Bev continued, "Phil said the Beckett's attorney hinted that they might accept the land and allow Phil to have—"

"But that can't be legal?" Nana Cole interrupted. "Making a change like that."

"If the will were thrown out entirely The Conservancy would get nothing. Rupert Beckett would get it all. If we agree, then Phil would give us a sizeable donation."

"Wait," I said, swallowing another bite of cake. "This doesn't sound like hinting. This sounds like a full-on negotiation."

Seriously, I'd had enough one-night stands in West Hollywood to recognize a negotiation when I heard it. Bev simply nodded and sipped her coffee.

"All of this would fall apart if we could prove the Becketts killed Sammy," I said.

"Oh, but they couldn't possibly," Nana Cole said. "I'm sure it was this Phil person trying to get his hands on Sammy's money."

"I really don't think so," was my wimpy answer.

But I had to wonder if I was just defending Phil because he was gay. Given everything I'd learned about Sammy: his establishing the AIDS clinic, his helping guys who'd been arrested cruising, his disco, well… he'd done a lot for gay people in the area. It was terrible to think he might have been killed by one. It seemed like it would confirm everything bigots thought. It *shouldn't*. I mean, straight people kill all the time. In fact, they commit almost *all* the murders, and no one ever says their sexuality had anything to do with it.

"More coffee?" Nana Cole asked.

"No, thanks."

"You haven't had any breakfast."

"I just ate a piece of coffee cake."

"Let me make you some eggs."

"Later. Right now I need to take a shower."

I wasn't all the way up the stairs when I took my flip phone out of my pocket. I went through the contact list and found Detective Lehmann. *Who'd have thought I'd have a sheriff's deputy in my contact list?* I giggled at the idea.

"Sheriff's Department," a woman said.

"Yes, Detective Lehmann please."

Then I waited. And waited. The woman came back. "Who are you waiting for?"

"Detective Lehmann."

"Right. One second."

Then I was back on hold. Waiting.

"Hello?" Lehmann finally came to the phone. "Who is this?"

"Henry Milch."

"What do you want?"

I wanted the reward, but I think I'd already made that clear. "I think I know who killed Sammy Hart. Rupert Beckett and his son, Rupert Beckett."

"Oh yeah, why do you think that?"

"They're contesting Sammy's will. They're trying to get the land he left to The Conservancy. It's worth, like, a lot." I had no idea how much it was really worth. I wanted to say millions but that would be California pricing.

"Uh, well, that doesn't really mean anything."

"But, that would be why Bev was implicated. To weaken The Conservancy's—"

"The day Sammy was killed both of the Becketts were downstate. St. Joseph's County. They'd hired some Amish carpenters to do some kitchen cabinets for them. They went down to pick it up. Stayed overnight in Kalamazoo."

"Have you confirmed that?"

"Of course, I've confirmed that." He was getting bristly. I suspected he was losing patience with me.

"Because you can't just call the Amish on the phone."

"Yes, I'm fully aware of that. I called the sheriff down there. He went out and talked to the carpenter the Becketts bought from. Their alibi is legit. Okay?"

"But they have the best motive. There's a lot of money at stake."

"That's not the only reason people kill."

"Well, I know that."

"And murderers don't always have good reasons. Think about it. If it was a good idea to kill, wouldn't more people do it?"

He had me there. The very nature of murder—which was almost always a bad idea—meant that reasonableness shouldn't always be considered when trying to understand it. Since it was a bad idea to kill Sammy, the reason he was killed might also be a bad idea.

"Is that all?" Lehmann asked.

"Um, yeah, I guess so."

"Good."

He hung up. That left me wondering what to do next. I mean, if murder was illogical how does anyone ever figure it out? I'd been looking for connections, cause and effect, one thing that would lead to another… but maybe that was wrong. Maybe what I needed to look at were things that didn't connect, that didn't belong together. Things no one would suspect.

———

OPAL PARKED the ladybug at a meter and got out to pump a bunch of quarters into it. It was twenty to four, so we were there in plenty of time. Chris Caine wasn't there yet so we walked into Drip together. I'd considered suggesting that we not do that, but knew I'd get my head ripped off. Especially since...

At Nana Cole's, I'd gotten into the passenger side of Opal's car and taken a quick look at her.

"Don't say a word," she said without looking at me.

It was hard, but I kept my mouth shut. She was wearing a heavy brown woolen skirt, scrunchie boots, a plaid jacket in autumn tones and an orange cowl neck sweater. She looked like a middle-aged art teacher. Even with her hair, which was now, suddenly, electric green.

"When I started working at Pastiche, I was given several outfits. I'm supposed to wear them. All right?"

"I'm not saying anything."

"Good. Don't."

And then she jumped because my grandmother was knocking on her window. At first I thought I must have forgotten something, but then why would she be knocking—

Opal buzzed the window down.

"You're not selling my grandson drugs, are you?" Nana Cole asked. I dropped my head into my hands.

"I don't sell drugs. Besides, he can find them on his own."

"What? What does that mean?"

"It means they're all over the place. Do you think drugs are hard to get?"

"Nana, she's teasing you. Drugs are illegal. They're hard to get. Really hard to get. Okay?"

"Is that all?" Opal asked. "We're going to be late."

"Late for what?"

Opal ignored that and zipped the window up. Glowering, Nana Cole stepped away from the car. She hugged herself against the cold since she'd come out without a coat. It was starting to snow and the flakes melted on the windshield.

Heading down the driveway, Opal said, "Your grandmother thinks you're a drug addict."

"That doesn't mean anything. She thinks George Bush is a genius and Pat Robertson is a saint."

Opal shrugged. I had an obvious a point.

When we got to Drip, I ordered a giant latte, and a blueberry and cream cheese muffin. Opal got a soy mocha and a gluten-free cookie. I was starting to realize something about Wyandot County. Surprisingly, there were a lot of the crunchy, hippy types you'd expect to find in California; and, not quite as surprising, there were also a lot of right-wing wackos like you'd find in Alabama. It was like living in Cali-bama.

"What are you thinking about?" Opal asked. "You have a weird look on your face."

"I'm going to sit over there," I said, pointing at a table for two near the front window. "Don't sit too close."

"But—"

I raised a finger to silence her. She glared at me as I went to sit by the window. There really wasn't any reason she couldn't have sat with me, other than the fact that I wanted to do this on my own. I mean, I was not what Chris was expecting so adding a girl to the mix didn't really change anything.

When we'd set up the time, Chris had promised to wear a red sweater so I'd know him. He was expecting me to be a gray-haired fifty-five-year-old. I looked around the coffee shop. Luckily, there weren't any guys who looked like that. I kept my eyes on the door, watching people come in. Two giggling girls in their late teens, a wannabe serial killer clutching a laptop, a woman in her sixties meeting three others for mah-jongg, and finally, a really sexy guy in his late thirties wearing a red sweater.

I glanced at Opal and raised my eyebrows; she raised hers back. Chris went up to the counter and ordered a coffee. An actual coffee not a coffee drink. He took his cup of coffee and sat down at the table next to me. I hopped over.

"Hello."

"I'm waiting for someone."

"You're waiting for me. I'm Henry."

"I'm waiting for someone named Richard."

"Yeah, I kind of lied."

"You're not my type."

"Yeah, I lied about that too."

"I don't like liars," said the man who cheated on his wife. Well, maybe he cheated. She said she knew so maybe—didn't matter.

"I'm the person who found Sammy Hart's body."

"Okay."

"And you were seeing him."

He narrowed his eyes at me. "You're the little snot who was harassing my wife."

Okay, so their relationship was more honest than I'd thought. And neither of them really liked me.

"You were involved with Sammy; did he say anything to you that might have to do with his death?"

His jaw tightened. "You mean like, 'I think so and so is going to kill me?' No."

"It doesn't have to be that specific."

"No."

This wasn't going well. Had I just wasted my time? But then I had a thought. "You said you were in construction."

"I am. You want a new kitchen?"

"Are you a carpenter?"

"Among other things."

"You have your own business?"

"No, I work for Beckett Construction."

"You work for Rupert Beckett—*senior*."

"Senior doesn't come in much. I work mostly for Rupert Jr."

"There's a property on Goose Lake that they want to get a hold of. Do you know anything about that?"

He got quiet, picked at a chip in the table's varnish, then sipped his coffee. "It's not specifically about that."

"What's it specifically about?"

"Sammy was thinking about creating a trust. Instead of a will. It would have made things harder to contest."

"So, he was expecting his will to be contested?"

"He knew it was possible. Even likely. The Ruperts felt they were entitled to the Goose Lake land. They actually—they'd found out Sammy was HIV positive. They were waiting for him to die."

"But I was told the land came through Sammy's father, who wasn't a Beckett."

"That's true, but his mother owned it for twenty years. They figured that made it Beckett land. And that they were entitled to it."

I decided to change directions slightly. "What about Phil? He was Sammy's boyfriend."

"They didn't live together."

"He left everything to Phil. Was the trust going to be different?"

"Things had cooled down with Phil. Sammy wanted me to leave my wife. He wanted to make me part of the trust."

Okay, that was explaining some things. First, Audrey was right, she was losing her husband. It also explained why Phil never mentioned the trust—or did it?

"Did Phil know about the trust?"

"I don't think so. He would have known eventually, of course."

"Did he know about you?"

"I don't think so."

"What about Richard?"

"Richard, the librarian?"

"Yes."

"What about him?"

"Sammy was seeing him too."

"No, he wasn't."

"Are you sure? I mean, Sammy didn't tell Phil about you."

"Sammy would never have gone out with Richard. He's too old. Sammy liked younger guys. Like me."

Chapter 23

"SO- WHAT DID HE SAY?" Opal was racing us back to Masons Bay at about ten miles over the speed limit. Snow had begun to fall in earnest. It came at us like swirling confetti.

"Should you be driving this fast? It's snowing pretty hard."

"I've lived here forever. I know how to drive in this weather. What did that guy say?"

I considered a moment, and said, "Tell me more about Richard."

"Richard? Why?"

"Sammy liked younger guys, is that true?"

"I don't know. I've never understood what attracts gay men to each other."

Seriously? I thought. Had she never seen a Falcon video? Actually, probably not.

"Chris is much younger than Sammy was. And Phil was about ten or fifteen years younger. Richard is about his same age though."

"Why is that important?"

"Chris just said that Sammy would never have been seeing Richard. Not his type."

"You think Richard lied to me?"

"Probably, but why? Why would he lie about that?"

We drove in silence for a bit. I really had no idea why

Richard would tell that particular lie. To make himself more important? Or maybe to cover up—

"Did you notice anything about Sammy and Richard's friendship in the months before Sammy was killed?"

"No, not really. I mean, I barely saw them together. I mean, maybe they weren't as friendly… but when Richard told me they were seeing each other that made sense because—oh, you think he lied to cover that up."

"I do."

I could have mentioned that I'd seen Richard at Ronnie Sheck's trailer, but I didn't want to remind her—

"You think Richard killed Sammy," she said.

"I don't want to think that."

"No, me neither."

Andrew Cunanan, Jeffery Dahmer, John Wayne Gacy. Honestly, I hated the idea that anyone gay ever murdered anyone. And it wasn't fair that I and every other minority felt like we had to take responsibility for these people. Bad people came in all varieties. Still, even before we were sure, I felt twinges of embarrassment and shame.

Opal's purse sat on the cupholders in front of the gear shift. She leaned over and began digging around in it. The plastic rose in the dashboard vase scraped at her forehead.

"What are you doing? Look at the road."

She sat up and looked at the road. "What? It's not doing anything." Having found her flip phone during her dive into the purse, she tossed it in my lap. "Call Pastiche. Tell them I'm in the bathroom vomiting."

"Really?"

"Richard lied to me. We're going to find out why."

I flipped through her contact list and found the number for Pastiche. When a woman answered I said, "Hi, I'm calling for Opal—" I realized I did not know her last name. "Um, she's in the bathroom vomiting. She not going to make it tonight."

"All right," the woman's voice was tight. She didn't believe me.

"Should I have her call you when she gets better?"

"No, just tell her I'll see her tomorrow at five." And then she hung up on me.

I told Opal, "She'll see you tomorrow at five."

"But I'm not—oh, I guess I am. I hope it's only a twenty-four-hour bug." And then she pulled a really scary U-turn at an empty intersection. I thought the ladybug might skid off the road.

Wyandot District Library was a recent two-story building of brick and glass with a spectacular view of Lake Michigan and a parking lot in front—which was nearly empty. The snow had begun to collect; there were a couple of inches on the ground. We couldn't actually see Lake Michigan, it was behind a curtain of white.

When we got out of the car, the wind had the eerie sound of an earthquake, except this was more like an earthquake zooming right passed us. Repeatedly. I pulled my coat tight around me. "Jesus. What the fuck?"

"Lake effect."

"The wind?"

"The snow, dummy."

Once we got into the library, we stomped the snow off our feet and hurried by the circulation desk at the front.

"Where are we going?" I asked.

"Richard works in children's books."

Oh my God, I thought, an aging, homosexual drug addict is the children's librarian? Even I thought that was a bad idea. I followed Opal; she seemed to know where she was going. The kids' section was in the back corner of the first floor. Tucked against one wall was a gray metal desk that had been decorated with dinosaur stickers and smiley faces. There were no children around. Richard sat behind the desk, chin on his chest, snoring. He looked old, thin and faintly yellow.

"He's dying," I said, not thinking.

Opal stared at me, then at him.

"Richard?"

He woke with a start. "What? Who?"

"Richard, you lied to me about Sammy. You weren't seeing him. Not in the way you said."

He looked us, like a little boy caught playing with matches.

"No, he wasn't my boyfriend."

"You never had sex with him," I clarified.

"Uh—no."

"Why did you tell me that?" Opal demanded.

"I dunno."

"I think you do."

"Honestly?"

"No, lie to me some more."

"I thought, okay maybe it's stupid, but I've been having money problems, I asked Sammy for help… but he turned me down. I thought if I told you we were together that it would get back to Phil and he'd, he'd want to help me. Financially."

"You told me not to tell him."

"I didn't think you'd pay any attention to that."

"Why did Sammy turn you down?" I asked. Everything I'd learned about him suggested he was generous. With strangers. With friends. So why—

Richard chuckled. "He said it was for my own good. He said giving me money would be like killing me."

"What are you talking about?" Opal asked. "That doesn't make—"

"He's been buying Oxy from Ronnie Sheck," I told her. "Probably for a long time."

Opal looked at him, then her eyes widened as though she suddenly saw him.

"Richard, did you kill Sammy?" I asked. Well, you never know, someone might say yes.

He shook his head. "No, no, I didn't."

"Did you know that Sammy was planning to put his estate into a trust?"

"Yes. I knew that."

"Did he tell you?"

He shook his head. "Phil told me."

"Phil— Did he kill Sammy?"

"No—that can't—"

I glanced at Opal, a tear ran down her cheek. She'd spent weeks worried about Sammy, doing everything she could to find him, and she'd done it with Richard and Phil. Now it seemed they'd both lied to her, they were both different men than she'd thought.

God, I thought, she was cynical and disillusioned before. What would she be now?

"Come on," she said. "Let's get out of here."

We walked out of the library and somehow the snow had gotten worse. With all the wind, it was beginning to form tiny drifts. Well, maybe not so tiny. There were patches where there was nothing and stretches where it was, like, ten inches deep. It was also getting into my orthopedic boot and my toes were fricking freezing.

When I got to the ladybug, I opened the passenger door and a shower of snowflakes flew in and landed all over the seat. I struggled into the car and closed the door behind me. Opal sat behind the steering well. I could tell by the look on her face she was devastated.

"I can't believe Phil did it. Phil killed him, didn't he?"

"What was his alibi for that day?"

"I don't know. I mean, I didn't go around asking my friends for alibis." She thought for a moment. "I suppose he was at his store."

"Or he said that. He seems to close the store whenever he feels like it and no one's going to remember it being closed for a couple of hours in February."

She dug around in her purse. Thankfully, we weren't moving. After finding her phone, she flipped it open and hit a few buttons before handing it to me. "You talk to him, I'm too upset."

Before I could ask "Who?" I heard someone, a man, on the phone saying, "Hello? Hello?"

I put the phone to my ear and said, "Hello?"

"Who is this? Where's Opal?"

It was Phil. I recognized his voice. "Um, she can't come to

the phone. She's driving."

"Okay. That's weird. She calls me when she's driving all the time."

"Oh, um, well, you know, the blizzard."

"Blizzard? What blizzard?"

"We're in Bellflower. In a blizzard."

"I'm in Ann Arbor, at a book fair. It's cloudy but not snowing."

"He's in Ann Arbor," I said to Opal.

"Why are you calling?" Phil asked.

"Uh, we, we're kind of stuck in Bellflower and wanted to know if we could come over and wait out the storm."

"You can wait it out at Sammy's house. The key is under the mat, which I guess means it's under the snow by now."

"Okay, well thanks," I said. "I have to go now. Bye."

I hung up.

Opal gave me a look, "Why didn't you ask him about Sammy?"

"My geography's not great, but isn't Ann Arbor right there by Canada? If he knows we think he killed Sammy, he could leave the country in like twenty minutes."

"Good point. I'm not really—"

She turned the car on and said, "Put on Damien Rice."

"Who?"

"The CD."

We pulled out of the library's parking lot. Sounds were muffled by the deepening snow. For once, Opal was driving slowly. I found the CD and slipped it into the slot. As soon as the sound began, Opal reached over and flipped forward two songs. I looked at the CD to see what was about to play: "The Blower's Daughter."

The song began slowly, barely more than the guy's voice.

"So, what's a blower? Is that a reference to oral sex?"

"Shut up. It's soothing."

We drove in silence for a while. The song, whose words had nothing to do with our situation, was mournful and serious. More depressing than soothing. Exactly the kind of music

I could never stand. It did match the look on her face, though.

And then I had that weird feeling, not déjà vu exactly, more like the feeling I was in a movie. The music, the snow, the super serious look on a green-haired girl as she leaned forward, concentrating on the road. I was in a movie and not a good one, not one with a hero who'd swing off a building and save us from the snow and our, well, Opal's murderous friend. No, we were kind of stuck having to make sense out of things that probably weren't going to make sense.

Okay, *that* was depressing. I hadn't had an Oxy all day and when I skipped a day—which I did a lot by the way—I did sometimes get a teensy bit depressed. And sometimes a runny nose.

"Do you have any tissues?" I asked Opal.

She looked over at me like I was from a different planet. "In the glove compartment."

I opened it and found the tissues, wiped my nose, and thought, *As soon as I get home I need to call Detective Lehmann.* I had to be the one to tell him Phil had killed Sammy. I mean, it was probably Richard and Opal who controlled the reward, but I wanted, needed, Detective Lehmann on my side. I thought about gently prodding Opal to see if I'd qualified yet, but she looked really, really intense as she drove us back to Masons Bay.

I tried to figure out where we were. Believe it or not I'd begun to recognize landmarks, so I might have had some idea where we were if I'd been able to see anything.

"How much longer?"

"We're almost to Masons Bay."

"Okay. Where do you live, by the way?" I'd never asked and felt like maybe I was kind of a jerk for that.

"Coldwater."

"Where is that?"

"Twenty, twenty-five minutes inland."

"Oh. You should stay until the snow stops at least," I said, though I regretted it immediately.

"I'll be fine."

"You want to risk the ladybug?" I asked. It would not be the end of the world if she totaled the car, but I knew that anyone who painted dots on a car and glued eyelashes to its headlights liked their car too much to risk it.

When she didn't say anything, I said, "I hope you're hungry, my nana will try to feed you."

"I could eat," she said reluctantly.

Not like she'll have a choice. And then, a minute or two later, we were turning down Nana Cole's long dirt driveway. The ladybug was struggling; the snow in the driveway must have been six inches deep. They wouldn't come to plow until the storm stopped and who knew when that would happen.

Opal pulled in next to the pole garage and turned off the car. The wind roared around us as we got out, the snow well above our ankles. I couldn't help myself saying, "This is crazy." And it was. We'd had several snow storms since I'd been there, but this was by far the worst and that didn't even make sense to me since it was so late in the season.

As we walked toward the kitchen door, I called out for Reilly. I wasn't sure he'd be able to hear me since it felt like the wind was swallowing my calls.

"Nana!" I called out once inside.

I heard movement in the other room and a moment later she was in the living room.

"I was watching *9&10 News*."

"You remember Opal," I said.

"We haven't actually met."

"Oh, well, this is Opal," I said. Opal waved at Nana who almost, not quite, smiled. "The roads are bad. She's going to wait out the storm."

"We're not having anything fancy for dinner. Just some venison chili and cornbread."

"That sounds wonderful," Opal said. I wasn't so sure. Every time Nana Cole said venison all I heard was Bambi.

"Is Reilly inside?" I asked.

Nana Cole shook her head. "Haven't seen him for a while."

Neither Opal nor I had made a move to take off our coats

and boots. I looked at her and said, "Go ahead and make yourself comfortable. I'm going to look for Reilly."

"I was brought up that a dog is an animal and animals belong outside," Nana Cole said to Opal. "He acts like I'm Hitler because I put my dog out."

"I thought he was *my* dog?" I asked and didn't wait for an answer.

Back out in the snow and wind, I tromped out toward the gardens toward the doghouse. It was entirely possible Reilly was in there and simply couldn't hear me. I kept calling for him, "Reilly! Reilly!" The drifts were now half way up my calf in places. It was getting harder and harder to get around, especially since one of my feet was in a regular boot and the other was a huge disaster. My toes were freezing, snow was getting in everywhere and beginning to melt. This was probably not such a great idea.

I called for my dog a few more times, then decided to give up and go inside. When I turned around, expecting to see the ladybug sitting in the driveway, instead I saw that it was obscured by a big gray, SUV—a Land Rover—with a wide scrape of red paint on the side. It was Sammy's Land Rover—and that meant Phil had lied, he wasn't in Ann Arbor. He was right here in Nana Cole's driveway.

And now I was absolutely certain, Phil had killed Sammy.

Chapter 24

THROUGH THE BLOWING SNOW. I saw a man in a heavy parka standing near the kitchen door. Phil, except the glimpse of his face I could see didn't look like Phil, it was someone younger, but I couldn't see who until he stepped forward and turned slightly. Rupert Beckett Jr.

"What are you doing with Sammy's car?" I yelled over the wind.

"I took the other set of keys," he yelled back.

Other set of keys? Oh, right, cars came with two sets. Most people shared them, gave them to a husband, wife, boyfriend— my mother had the other set of keys to my, well her, Honda. Sammy probably just kept his other set in a drawer in his house. And that made me say, "When you killed him? You took the keys when you killed him?"

He smiled.

It made sense. No one thought to check for the extra set. Why would they?

"But you have an alibi. You were downstate."

"My cousin Rupert from over in Kalkaska went down with my dad. All they asked was whether there were two Ruperts."

"Why are you here? You just want to confess?"

He shook his head violently. "I came to kill you."

I looked at his hands; they were empty. "How?" If nothing else I had a right to know that. Right?

"Found it!" a voice behind me called out. I turned and saw Rupert Beckett Sr. coming out of the workshop. My grand-mother's hunting rifle in one hand.

"And I found the other thing we're looking for," Junior replied.

Rupert Sr. raised the rifle and pointed it me. "Now you're going to do what I say, you hear me?"

Doing what he wanted seemed like a very bad idea. I mean, Rupert Jr. had already told me they were going to kill me so why should I cooperate? Wouldn't I be better off—

"Let's go in the house."

Oh my God, I hadn't thought, hadn't realized, they were going to kill all three of us. I couldn't let that happen.

"I don't get it. What's the plan?" I did already get it, kind of, but asking stupid questions bought me time. And I needed it to figure out—

"You're going to kill them and then kill yourself," Rupert Jr. said gleefully. "You tried to kill yourself before, right?"

"That was an accident," I said, stubbornly. I just hated that no one believed me and now it was going to get me killed.

"All right, into the house."

"No."

"What do you mean no?"

"I mean I'm not going to help you get away with my murder. That would be kind of dumb, wouldn't it?"

"No, it would be smart to do as I say."

"Really? Why?"

"Do you want me to shoot you right here?"

"Okay. I mean, if the whole point of this is to make it look like I killed the women in the house and myself your shooting me here is going to screw that up."

"You're not hearing me. I'm going to *kill* you."

"And you're not hearing me. I'm going to make sure you go to jail for killing me."

The look on Rupert Sr.'s face was priceless. It had never

occurred to him that I might actually try to screw up his plan. I guess he thought I'd be so scared that I'd do whatever he said.

And here's the thing. Almost dying—like I nearly did in L.A.—makes it that much easier to get close to that particular flame. Maybe I was seconds away from Rupert pulling the trigger and maybe I wasn't.

What I did know was that if his plan was going to work he'd have to shoot me from the correct angle, one that I could get into all by myself, something I could make very difficult for him.

In all honesty, I was a little high. Adrenaline was flooding my body and who knows what else. Standing this close to death, well, it was almost as good as a couple of Oxy.

And then, totally unexpected, Reilly came bounding out of the snow and jumped—not on me, but on Rupert Sr. As he fell sideways, the rifle raised upward and went off. I screamed—sort of an *ugh* sound, very primal—and jumped on him while trying to pull the weapon away from him. A second later, Rupert Jr. jumped on me

Another shot, but not from the shotgun. Rupert Jr. rolled off me and I rolled off Rupert Sr. I looked up and there was my grandmother in the doorway holding some kind of handgun. I should have known she had a gun in the house. Guns were like potato chips to Nana Cole, she couldn't stop at just one.

"Rupert Beckett drop that rifle or I'll shoot your balls off. And you know I'm a good enough shot to do it."

Opal popped up behind Nana Cole, and said, "The sheriff is on his way."

Nana Cole came down the stoop, saying, "Henry, come in the house. I don't want you to catch your death."

Not sure whether she was making a joke or not—I was, after all, freezing my ass off—I got up and limped over. As I climbed the stoop into the kitchen, she said, "And you have a lot of explaining to do."

I decided it was a good time to use the two words I almost never said to her: "Yes, ma'am."

The sheriff arrived about ten minutes later, which was a

good thing since I think my grandmother was running out of excuses to not go ahead and just shoot them. I mean, they *were* trespassing, and she could probably have gotten away with it. Particularly after everyone found out they were murderers. They were also distant relatives—well, less distant to her than me. And shooting relatives, while common in this part of the country and most others now that I think about it, still resulted in a heavy dose of social stigma.

So anyway, the sheriff arrived. Nana Cole put her gun away, Opal freaked out because I almost got her killed then swore she'd never give me another ride as long as she lived, and the Ruperts were duly arrested for murder and attempted murder. I kept pointing out that it was two counts of attempted murder. Seriously, they'd tried to kill me twice and I wanted credit for it.

———

TWO DAYS later the snow was miraculously gone. The temperature had risen into the high forties, and the sky was even a pretty blue for a while. There had been a little bit of discussion about whether I could have the reward now or whether I'd have to wait until there was an actual conviction. Of course, the Ruperts confessed—well, sort of. Rupert Jr. turned state's evidence against his father about thirty seconds before Rupert Sr. tried to return the favor. In the confusion—neither was patient enough to wait for a lawyer—they'd managed to spill most of the beans without a deal.

I called Vinnie to let him know I was coming home, and he was less than enthusiastic.

"I suppose you can stay on the sofa for a little while."

It was not a very nice sofa. We'd inherited it from one of the bartenders at the restaurant where Vinnie worked. Vinnie liked to say that the sofa, like its previous owner, had been sat on one too many times.

"I thought you hated your roommate."

"I did hate him. But I can't just throw him out."

"*Did* hate him?" I said, picking up on the way he'd said that. "You don't hate him now?"

"Not as much."

"Oh my God, you're sleeping with him."

"Don't be ridiculous. I make him go back to his own room after we're done. I have absolutely no interest in *sleeping* with him."

"But—" I said, and then stopped. This had all gotten a lot harder. I needed a place to live. I wanted my old room back and suddenly that was not a possibility. All I had was sofa rights for "a little while," and then I would have to find another living situation.

"I was a good roommate, wasn't I?"

"Except for the part you took too many drugs and almost died, you were a peach."

"Ask around and see if anyone needs a roommate—and leave out the part about my almost dying. Okay?"

"Absolutely, darling."

After I hung up, I promised myself it wasn't going to be a problem. I thought about taking an Oxy—I still had eight in my stash—but decided it would be better to save them for a rainy day. Or rather, a rainier day.

I planned on getting my old job back making lattes and such. There might be another barista who needed a roommate. And then, of course, I could go to the LGBT Center and check their bulletin boards. Actually, I could go to their website and—

"Lunch!" Nana Cole yelled up the stairs. Reilly and I hurried downstairs. The boot was getting easier to maneuver. And when I took it off to take a shower, I could almost rest my full weight on that foot. Almost.

I sat down in front of a lunch of black bean soup and cheesy cornbread. Nana Cole sat across from me in front of her own lunch. I took a sip of soup followed by a bite of cornbread. While I was chewing, Nana Cole said, "I understand you're getting a reward."

"I am."

"And then you'll be leaving."

"That's the plan."

"That's what all the running around has been about? Getting that reward."

"Yes."

"I thought you were back on drugs."

"I wasn't ever *on* drugs. I like to have fun sometimes, relax. It's the same thing as you having a glass of wine. You drink wine but you're not an alcoholic."

"It's not the same thing though. I can't commit suicide with a bottle of wine."

"I wasn't trying to kill myself. How many times do I have to say that? It was an accident and my roommate kind of freaked out. I would have been fine if he'd left well enough alone."

"That's not what your mother said."

"Well, you know what she's like."

She was silent. I took another sip of soup. It was really good. I have to say, the one thing I would miss about Nana Cole was her cooking. The only thing. Then I decided I'd better change the course of this conversation before Nana Cole thought up something else to say on the subject.

"Are you upset that it was your cousin who killed Sammy?" I asked.

Okay, so yes, they were both cousins, but then I hardly had to explain the family relationships to her.

"Sammy was always trouble. But, yes, it is upsetting. I thought for sure it was one of Sammy's pansy friends who killed him. That would have made more sense."

A sudden jolt of white-hot anger over the word 'pansy' ripped through me. It was totally silly though since Vinnie and I used silly words like that. I mean, we made jokes about pansies and fruits and maricons all the time. We even used more offensives words. But the thing was we never meant anything by it. But Nana Cole... she meant something by it and that was the part that made me so mad.

"You just said Sammy was trouble."

"Yes, but you know those people have no morals."

"You mean the Becketts."

"No, I mean queers."

"It's you. It's people like you."

"I don't know what you're talking about."

"You call people names, you judge them, you say they're immoral, you believe they do terrible things even though you have no idea. It's people like you who give the Rupert Becketts of the world permission. You make it okay for them to hurt us, to kill us. You're every bit as responsible."

I wasn't quite sure where this was coming from. I mean, it sounded like something Sammy would say or, rather, what I imagined Sammy would say.

"Us? What do you mean, us?"

"Yes, Nana, I'm gay. Kind of stupid of you not to notice." I cringed after I said that. I mean, I'd just told her she was complicit in all violence against gay people and called her stupid in the space of thirty seconds. This was not going to be good for our relationship.

"No, no you can't be," she said. "Ith wong, ith agin Gaw."

She stopped speaking. Even she could hear that she'd begun to slur her words. Raising her right hand to her face she touched the left side and said, "Tingle."

"Nana! You're not all right," I said, stating the obvious. "I think we need to call an ambulance."

Abandoning my lunch, I went over to the wall phone near the entrance to the dining room. I quickly dialed 911—well, I tried to do it quickly. It was one of those ancient rotary phones and it seemed like it was taking forever. Finally, the operator came on.

"I think my grandmother is having a stroke."

"Where are you, dear?"

"2525 West Shore Road."

"Is she ambulatory?"

"Um, yes. I think so. She's slurring her speech and says that she's tingling."

"Okay, the rescue squad for Mason Bay is out on a call. They can be there in approximately twenty-five minutes. Do you want them to come? Or can you get your grandmother to the hospital on your own?"

"Oh God." I wasn't sure what to do. We could be at the hospital in Bellflower in twenty minutes, but I couldn't drive with a huge plastic boot on. Could I?

"Okay. I'm going to try. I may call you back in five minutes. Okay?"

"Of course. Good luck."

I went back over to the table and asked, "Can you stand up?"

She tried. I noticed right away her left arm and leg weren't cooperating. I helped her up. There seemed to be much less of her than I'd thought. I grabbed the keys off the hook by the door. I didn't bother with boots or coats or anything, we just walked out the back door and over to the Escalade. Reilly was right behind us.

I opened the passenger door and practically lifted Nana Cole in, clicked on her seatbelt, and then closed the door. I opened the back door and let Reilly jump in. That resulted in a few slurred words from the front seat—Reilly never got to ride in the car. I ignored them.

Walking around the SUV, I climbed into the driver's seat and put the keys in. There was no way I could drive with the boot on, so I bent over and un-Velcro-ed it. After easing it off, I threw it in the back seat. I put the Escalade in gear and slowly pressed on the gas. It wasn't terrible, but it wasn't good. I was going to have to use both feet to drive. With my right, messed up ankle I could gently press the gas. I'd have to use my left for the brake. Especially if I had to brake suddenly.

Turning the Escalade around, I headed down the driveway.

"Stay calm, Nana. We'll be at the hospital in twenty minutes. Everything's going to be okay."

She made a sound I couldn't decipher. Out on the 22, I eased the speed of the Escalade up until we were going about fifteen miles over the speed limit. I put the hazards on just in case we encountered one of the sherriff's deputies. I didn't want to stop, but if I had to I wanted it to be fast. Luckily, we weren't stopped. On the way, I kept trying to say reassuring things to Nana Cole—definitely a new experience.

I ran two red lights and honked at a few drivers as I passed them. By the time we reached the Bellflower city limits my ankle was throbbing and Nana Cole had stopped making any noise. When I got to Bellflower, fortunately there were signs leading me to the hospital. I'd noticed them before but had not given them a second thought.

Midland Hospital was a compound of buildings, mostly square, brick and only a few stories tall. I saw the sign for Emergency and swerved to follow it. Seconds later, I came to a stop. Jumped out of the car. Hopped around to the passenger side. Threw the door open. Nana Cole was slumped over. Unresponsive. I turned, scurried through the automatic doors and as soon as I got inside began screaming, "HELP!"

Chapter 25

"WE'RE NOT GOING to know anything for sure, not for weeks possibly," Dr. Stewart explained to me in the waiting room.

He was still gorgeous, which was weird. I was talking about my nana's health with a man who was probably better suited to underwear modeling. Seriously, even if he was a great doctor he'd be an even greater model.

"But we've given her something to break down clots, as well as an anticoagulant, and a sedative to keep her calm and comfortable. She's got a fighting chance at a full recovery. It's good that you got her here as quickly as you did."

"How long will she be here?"

"As I said, there's a lot we don't know. Stroke patients are typically in the hospital for a week or even two. Then they go to a rehabilitation facility for at least another two weeks. Many patients continue to need help when they get home. There are *some* services available."

"But not everything."

"No, not everything."

I nodded. This was serious. The possibilities here seemed to range from bad to spectacularly bad. And I had no idea what it meant, particularly what it meant for me.

"Thank you, Dr. Stewart."

"I'll be around tomorrow if you have any questions."

As soon as he walked away, I took out my flip phone. I had to make a call I didn't want to make. Better to get it out of the way. I pressed the button and after two rings my mother answered, "Well, there you are. I thought you'd never call me."

"Nana had a stroke."

"Is she dead?"

"No."

"Thank God."

"They think she'll recover. They just… they don't know how long it will take and how well she'll get on. She's having trouble talking and I think she's paralyzed on one side."

"Poor thing. It's not permanent, though. Is it?"

"They're not sure. Mom, you need to come."

"But you said she'll recover."

"You still need to come."

"Oh… it's, um, not a good time," she said. "David just bought a boat and now we have boating parties scheduled with his clients all summer."

"It's April."

"You know summer starts earlier here."

"What does any of that have to do with you?"

"Well, he can't do it alone. He needs me."

"Is he paying you?"

"Don't be obtuse."

"Is he going to marry you?"

"I think three tries is enough, don't you? I'd be a fool to do it again."

"And arranging your life around a man without payment or marriage isn't foolish?"

"That's enough. This isn't a conversation about me. You called to talk to me about your nana. Get me the doctor's name and I'll speak with him directly."

"Someone has to be here for Nana."

"Well, of course darling—*You're* there."

"I'm planning to leave soon."

"Well, that doesn't work, now does it?"

For some reason, the thing that Opal said to me came to

mind. She'd said that I was twenty-four and no one forced me to do anything. That I made my own choices. I decided to make a choice.

"I'm not staying," I told my mother.

"Henry, you have to."

"No, I don't. She's *your* mother. You're the one who should be here taking care of her."

"You know how it is between us. We don't get on. If I was there I'd just make everything worse."

"She and I don't get on either." I left out that she'd had a stroke while we were arguing. Something I was trying hard not to feel guilty about, and not doing such a great job of it.

"You two get on just fine. She adores you."

"Seriously? If she does, she's been keeping it a secret."

"And you need to be there. It's been good for you."

"How would you know?"

"The only thing your nana and I can talk about is you. You're the only thing we ever agree on. We talk all the time— and it's always about you."

"It's time for me to go home. You need to come and take care of your mother or you need to hire someone who will. Someone other than me."

"Think about it, Henry."

"No. Call me if you need a ride from the airport," and with that, I hung up on her.

Furious, I walked back into the ER on my way to the bed where I left her. They'd said they were planning to bring her upstairs soon, so we were almost done with the ER. And I was glad of it. It was quiet and nothing like the emergency rooms in L.A., but I still didn't like it. Not at all.

Walking through the ER, I recognized a man sitting in one of the beds. I stopped and stared at him.

"Richard?"

He looked up at me.

"Overdose?" I asked quietly.

"Tempting, but no. Liver failure."

And, of course, as soon as he mentioned it, I saw it. He was yellow. His skin was tinged with the color. But it was his eyeballs that were most noticeable. Around the edges they were a bright, unnatural yellow.

"Good luck," I whispered and then continued on to my grandmother's bed.

That was not me and would never be me. Richard was an addict. I was just playing around. Yes, I'd been thinking about taking an Oxy or two when I got tucked in for the night. My ankle, which I'd gotten back into its boot, was throbbing so it would be medicinal. Actual pain relief.

While I was still around, I should hit up Dr. Blinski for a refill or two or a dozen. I had the feeling, probably correct, that he handed out scripts like candy at Halloween. I certainly didn't have a doctor like that in L.A. Of course, there all I had to do was walk into Rage and ask around. That was how I'd gotten into trouble. Some random guy had given me three 20s and I'd misjudged what twenty milligrams of Oxy could do—well, when you took three. I'd only ever had 10s.

No, I was not Richard. I never would be. Maybe I wouldn't take any Oxy at all when I got back to Los Angeles. I could do that. I was sure I could do that.

Standing next to Nana Cole, I watched her. She seemed to be breathing just fine. Resting like nothing was wrong with her. They'd taken her clothes and put her in a thin gown. She'd at least need a cardigan. I'd have to bring her one.

Should I bring Reilly with me to Los Angeles? I didn't know if I could afford him. But then, Nana Cole wouldn't be able to take care—and that reminded me. Reilly was in the car sleeping under a blanket. I'd brought him a cup of water about a half an hour before. Did he need to be—

Nana Cole opened her eyes, a lovely dark brown but hazy around the edges of the iris—brown eyes like my mother's. Like mine. With her right hand she reached out and grabbed my arm. There was fear in her eyes, naked fear.

Why was I being such an idiot? There was only one way everything was going to be fine. Someone had to take care of her. I could stand on my head threatening my mother and she wasn't going to do it. There was only me.

Yeah, I could walk away. Take the reward money and go back to L.A. Not care what happened to Nana Cole. But that would make me exactly what she thought I was: Immoral. Okay, so maybe our definitions of what that word really meant were vastly different, but I certainly didn't want to be that—not by my own definition.

"I'm here," I told her, placing my hand on hers. "I'm not going anywhere."

Not for a long time.

Also by Marshall Thornton

Full Release

The Ghost Slept Over

My Favorite Uncle

Femme

Praline Goes to Washington

Aunt Belle's Time Travel & Collectibles

Masc

Never Rest

Made in the USA
Middletown, DE
23 August 2021